Corinthian Spirit

by

M A Lucas

Content

FAITH

HOPE

LOVE

"Who'd ring at this time of night?" I say to myself, as I look across at the alarm clock and see the little hand pushing up toward the number twelve. It is Saturday night and I'd only just dropped off to sleep.

Please allow me to introduce myself. I'm Andy Roberts, a young free and single guy - well, the wrong side of thirty, but you wouldn't know to look at me. I landed myself a very nice job at the Theatre and a fashionable, cosy, little terraced house on the north side of town. Everything is going very nicely, thank you very much, and a phone call at this hour can only mean one thing; someone's in trouble.

"Andy. Thank God you're home."
This is a voice I know well … and it belongs to Liz. Not my favourite person right this minute but certainly a very valued friend.
"Oh, hi Liz. You ok?"
"I … I …", she splutters.
"That good, hey?"
In my half awake state, I quickly realise that attempted humour is not the right line to take.
Liz breaks down into tears and I listen to her sobs for a few seconds.
"Take your time. Just tell me where you are."
"I'm at … the Police Station." She enlightens me.
There's a pause. Liz can't speak and I'm trying to think.
"Ok. Are you … er, hurt? I mean, have you been attacked or anything?"
"No. I've been arrested. I didn't know who else to call. I'm sorry." She says.
"Don't be silly. You hang in there and I'll be with you in about ten minutes, ok?"
"Yeah. Great. Thanks." She affirms and with a last sniffle, she hangs up.

It's funny how sometimes you end up somewhere that you never expected to be - and the only reason you're there is that you happened to meet somebody who changes the whole direction of your life. Only a month ago, at Easter, I got off a train with my bags, an address and a hopeful feeling. Now I'm hurtling across town to talk to the Police in a city that I hardly know. The reason I'm here is Liz. The reason I'm speeding is Liz. Heck, I don't even know what she's supposed to have done.

I take my cup of coffee from the nice WPC and look out of the window, the black night lit by silent street lamps and think ... "how long are they gonna be?" It's already been a long time since I arrived, an hour or more. I think I'll take a step outside and get some air. If only I could get to speak to her I could maybe help in some way.

Liz had put me up for a while until I found a place of my own. Thankfully, it only took me a couple of weeks but it's been all go since then, getting myself sorted. I haven't been in touch with her for a week or more. I was thinking of dropping in on her this evening to see what she was up to. I dread to think how that might have turned out!

"How long is this going to take?" I enquire when I come back into the brightly lit reception.
The female officer behind the desk looks me in the eye with confidence and authority.
"Shouldn't be long now. I can check for you if you like." She says.
"That's ok. I'm not going anywhere. I would like to know why she's been brought in though. She wasn't up to saying anything when she rang.'
"I'm afraid I can't give you that information Sir." She tells me before adding, "She's being held under arrest and interviewed at the moment."

Right on cue, a man in plain clothes, presumably from CID, comes out to the desk and the two of them talk in hushed tones. At one point they both glance in my direction and I immediately feel under suspicion. I've only been in a Police Station once and that was only to assist with their enquiries. The law is one area that I willingly stay the right side of. Of course, we all end up breaking the law occasionally, don't we? But it's usually in a socially acceptable way, where nobody gets hurt: well, except in unforeseeable circumstances. Smoking the odd joint is about as rebellious as it comes with me. The detective leaves the desk with another parting glance at me.

"Mr Roberts." I am summoned to attend at the desk. "Mr Davies has advised me that Miss Simmons is to remain in custody and that you will be in able to see her briefly in a short while. You did say you were just a friend, didn't you?"
Now my head is reeling. "Er … yes. Well, we were once … yeah, don't suppose you needed to know that, eh?"
"No Sir. I'd take a seat if I were you." She says, as if giving me an order.

The twenty minutes that follow have that strange other worldliness that makes you unsure of how much time has actually passed. There is nothing to be done with it except think; it just passes and then, reality resumes.

"Would you like to step this way Sir?" the WPC enquires.

Would I? Yes, I think so. I follow my guide into the inner sanctum where everything seems very ordinary and matter of fact but it's an illusion; in fact, all is very unusual and unpredictable. I couldn't do this for a living. It's a calling, I'm sure. Suddenly aware that my friend has been embroiled in this scenario for a few hours I feel deep concern for her, whatever her crime may be.

A door is opened and held for me to proceed into the room. As I pass through it, Liz is slumped dishevelled and despondent at the far side of a desk. The door closes behind me and we are alone.

She wipes her eyes and smiles at me. Without bothering with the chair nearest to me I go round the desk, she stands and she engulfs me in a hug that has more emotion than most that I have known in my life.

"I've been so stupid Andy. SO stupid." She confesses.
"I'm sure that's not true. What have they got you on?"
She mumbles into my shoulder, "Coke. Possession. It wasn't even mine."

For the second time tonight, I am struggling for what to say next. Dragging the chair round the table I get Liz to sit down and place myself in front of her. It's my turn to wipe the hair from her face and a tear from her cheek. Looking directly into the beautiful but scared eyes I smile and it's good to see her smile back at me.

"I don't know how long we have but give me some details and I'll see what I can do. Trust me." I say to her in all sincerity.

We had a good time when we were together. We did some stuff, got a little too drunk, shared some weed and had great sex. Looking at her now, I just want to wrap her up in cotton wool and take her home with me. A casual relationship? I don't think so. Not for me at any rate. Unfortunately, great sex became ok sex and the fun times became just amusing moments. She needed to find a new fix. Maybe this was inevitable.

The story unfolds. A party, her new boyfriend Matt is a little bit worse for wear but wants a line. He makes a call to a guy but he's out of town having a few beers in a village pub. It's only a fifteen minute drive away so Matt gives her the cash and she jumps in the car. She could do with a line too to make the night just right.

Heading back on the A27, deal done, smiling a big smile and the Stone Roses blaring out of the stereo from the Beamer, it had to happen. A bored traffic cop clocks her at eighty five, the sirens wail and the lights flash. She should have thrown the bag out the window; she knows that but wasn't thinking. Couldn't believe she'd failed the test; hadn't thought she's be searched. It was as if they had a sixth sense and soon located the few grams of resin in her fag packet. A quick search of the car was all they needed to find the bag under the passenger seat.

She's an attractive young woman, speeding along in a flash car on a Saturday night. Who needs a sixth sense? Not these people. They know what's going on out there. They've got the statistics and the psychological profiles all on file. You're a sitting target Liz. I don't say this to her, obviously. She knows it but can't or won't take a look at it. Getting high on a Saturday night, that's all that matters.

God knows what will happen to her. It's not as if she has much of a defence. Defence! The word hits my brain like headlights coming over the brow of a hill and I realise that I'm the rabbit. The alarm bells in my head obviously resonate round the room because Liz asks me, "What's the matter?"
"Oh, nothing … it's just, I was wondering whether they asked you where you got it from and what that detective seargent's up to right now."
"Leave it out Andy. I said I'd BEEN stupid, not that I AM stupid!"
"They haven't shown much interest in me. No reason to, I suppose."
"I just wanna get out of here Andy."
"OK, it's probably best not to talk about it here. You try and hang in there and I'll be back first thing with the cavalry."

We hug and kiss goodbye and I even whisper that I love her. By her reaction, or lack of it, I imagine she takes this as a kind of brotherly love. If only she knew, if only. Leaving the room I find an officer standing outside and he escorts me out from whence I came. I breathe in the cool night air, trying not to think about the rough time Liz is enduring as she waits, like a watchman waits, for the dawn.

"Whoa!" Paranoia city or what? I'm gonna be looking over my shoulder for weeks. They know where I live and everything. Does Matt know? Where is that idiot? Yes, I'm jealous and now he's got the woman that I love in to trouble. Rather than go straight home, I grab some fags from an all night petrol station out on the by-pass. Once I've parked, I light up and start walking the quiet streets. It's nearly three o'clock but I'm no longer tired. There is a choice to be made. Do I sleep and hope that I can rouse myself in the morning or stay awake and try to form a plan?

Adrenaline is the strongest drug that there has ever been but sooner or later it cuts off. By the time I get indoors my body and soul are screaming out for the comforting embrace of the duvet so I crawl under it. I take my shoes off but that's as far as I get.

What I didn't remember to do was to set the alarm. On a Sunday morning all is peace and serenity in this part of the world. No whistling postman or thundering lorries. Again, it's the ring of the telephone that gets me up, like a sentry found asleep on duty. Its 10:38 and I think I made the wrong decision. To my surprise, it's Matt and in my semi-conscious state I aim to please.

"Got anything to tell me, 'av-ya mate?" Matt opens up with.
"Er ... yeah. I suppose you're wondering where Liz got to, right." I reply, not yet sure of where Matt is coming from.
"Well, that I know but you might av told me!"
I ramble on "Sure, right, sorry. It was all a bit scary. I was gonna ring you first thing after I spoke to ... oh, ****!"
"Ah, the penny drops ... to Liz, that's right." Matt says with a thick

slice of sarcasm.

"Have you spoken to her?" I ask.

"Yeah, I rang to see if there'd been in an accident or something and they told me they 'ad-er in custody. Went down there and sorted it. She's gonna be in Court so I need to get on to her brief in the morning. She don't want her old man to know, not just yet anyway."

Relieved, I answer "Oh, great. Looks like you handled it much better than I would have."

"Once you get to know the system it's not so hard. You're lucky you haven't had to." He tells me, almost boasting.

"Where is she now?"

"She's asleep next door. She did wonder where you were. I told her there was no point both of us rushing around." Matt nonchalantly explains.

"Thanks. I wouldn't want her to think I'd let her down: I owe you one." I tell him.

"Too right."

The tone of Matt's voice, as it trails away and the receiver clicks down, leaves me thinking that this is a favour that might be called in one day; probably sooner than later too. My bacon has been well and truly saved though, so I shouldn't begrudge it.

With the events of the last 24 hours swirling around my brain, I now have some time to myself and Sunday afternoon is the perfect time for some reflection.

I've already decided that Chichester is a good place to be. You just have to walk around to get the historical interest thing but it also has many other ways to stimulate the mind. I'm a little biased, I know. Living and working in the centre of town gives me a much better idea of what's going on around me. I was very lucky to get the job here. My official title, Assistant Manager, is a broad name for a very varied role. I've had to find my way around quite quickly and have already met a fair cross-section of people from the delightful to the altogether odd. The odd ones are mostly actors.

I should know because I wanted to be one myself but realised that I just wasn't dedicated enough to make it. I dabbled with drama at university, while studying English, but always felt I was destined for the backstage life. In fact, I thought I was going to be following a career in teaching until I met up with Liz last summer: more of that later.

So, following my light lunch, my study of the week's news is interrupted by the door bell. Matt's furrowed brow is probably in stark contrast to my smiling face but my cheerfulness seems to lift him and I'm aware of his facial muscles relaxing in reciprocation.
"Hi Andy, is it a good time?" he enquires.
"Sure, I was about to make some coffee, come on in."
"I've been thinking about what happened last night and was wondering if you fancied a chat." Matt replies.
I surmise from his rigid body language that he isn't coming in, "Actually, I could do with some fresh air if you know a good spot for a stroll."
"I know a good place out in the country or we could just go from here; up to you mate." He offers.
I decide, "Round the wall is easier on a lazy Sunday afternoon."

I have discovered much of Chichester's long and interesting history. The north side, where I live, is enclosed inside the old city wall which has now been assimilated by modern planning. There is much more of it all the way around: following the ring road, pretty much. It'll be a fair distance but I'll be glad of the opportunity and its neutral territory to talk about Liz's predicament.

Don't get me wrong, Matt seems like a reasonable guy but I hardly know him. I'm reading far too much into the situation and feeling weird about having carnal knowledge of his girlfriend. If we start analysing our lives, I expect there'd be an infinite number of reasons for doing what we do. Maybe that's where the problem lies; we all look at things from a different angle. Anyway, I just hope he doesn't ask me any awkward questions.

Our circular route begins just around the corner. Matt listens patiently to my account of the previous evening, nodding at bits, frowning at others. It was a real relief that he'd rung the cop shop this morning. I would have felt so bad about letting Liz down if he hadn't.

To see how his story fits around Liz's I enquire about his evening. Everything checks out for the part when they are together and it sounds as if he was really worried when she didn't come back to him. He'd rung his dealer to check that Liz had picked up the merchandise and hit the road, as arranged. After a mild panic and a reassuring call to the local hospital to check for emergency admissions, things start to become a little vague. By reading between the lines, it sounds as if he bottled out of ringing her parents because they are not overly keen on their lovely daughter getting involved with young Matthew. He said he didn't want to worry them unnecessarily but I think it's more likely that he feared their right and proper concern about darling Lizzie's drug running.

Slightly further back in the gloom of half truths is the nocturnal activities of my new friend with respect to the other twenty-four hour party people he was hanging out with. I know from personal experience that, man to man, it is hard to feel anything other than a little smug and self satisfied after a new conquest. During a pleasant spell on our walk, across a small but perfectly formed little park, he did sound a mite enthusiastic about a young lady named Claire. I've no wish to make false allegations, especially in view of my over-protective thoughts about my ex, BUT ... I reckon some bodily fluids may have been exchanged after some illegal substances had been taken.

After all of the night's exploits have been revealed and we are both fully acquainted with the facts, as given, there is a brief period of reflection as we walk on towards the area of the city where Liz resides. It's the first time on our walk that I have the idea to stop and take in the warm and relaxing feeling of the sun on my skin and to acknowledge the other pleasures afforded by my senses. With a renewed sense of confidence in our mutual understanding, I push the conversation on in an attempt to get some questions of my own onto the agenda.

"Matt, I'm not sure why she rang me instead of you. Did she say why?"
"I'm not surprised: she really trusts you mate." Matt replies with a very genuine ring to his tone.
"All the same, I'd be a bit miffed if I was in your shoes. Don't get the wrong idea here; anything there was with me and Liz is a thing of the past, you know that, right?" I hope that this sounds more reassuring to Matt than it smacks of desperation to me.

I should add that it may not be entirely true but it's how I intend to proceed in practice, which is what really matters, wouldn't you say?

"I guess so, Andy. I think she was trying to protect me. I wouldn't have been much help to her last night; much better to deal with it in the cold light of day." Matt elucidates and draws a deep, reflective breathe.

As we walk on and the familiar streets near my new home tell me that this tête-à-tête is nearing its conclusion, I get all I need to know about Liz's ordeal and eventual release on bail. As we part I try to encourage Matt not to worry and re-assure him that they could both rely on me to help see Liz through this. As he drove away I began to think that this was likely to mean obscuring the truth to some degree. When I closed the door of my flat and lent against it with some relief, I had no inkling of how many times I might have to walk those walls before all of this was over and done with.

For now, I needed a cold beer in my hands, my headphones over my ears and *The Streets* in the CD player. There are times when I need to be reassured of how the world is by recalling happy memories, stirred by favourite songs. I often reach for *Original Pirate Material* when I can feel that some serious grounding is required. I can't believe that I am the only person to have sought inspiration while listening to this collection of songs. They are songs that thrilled me one summer and will live with me forever.

I am unable to join in the chorus of *"Don't mug yourself"* without a wry laugh at myself; by the time the track's eerie final call to *Stay Positive* has finished assaulting my brain, I am lost in a stream of consciousness that is both delightful and troubling.

My first impression of Liz was not that good; I thought she was a bit full of herself to be honest. I soon came to realise that this was a defence mechanism and, although she did come from a privileged background with all she needed to make a good start in life, she was still young, vulnerable and far from home in the Lakes.

I wasn't at my best either. Let me explain.

Growing up in Great Yarmouth had not been a traumatic experience, but not particularly liberating either. I had no great ambitions that I was bursting to pursue but I coped commendably with the normal run of school life. As a result, I found myself at university in Canterbury. The two main joys that occupied most of my waking hours were reading and sailing. I was quite content to be studying English and dreaming of stashing away enough cash to buy my own boat afterwards.

I won't pretend that my student days were any less predictable than the pictures that you've probably already got in your head. Yes, I got drunk a lot. Yes, if I had spent less time contemplating the various options and strategies for sleeping with the girls on the course, I may have come away with a first. I spent a very good year with a blonde who was into Oasis. She was my wonderwall.

So, where was I? Right, I'm twenty one and its decision time. But I made a big mistake. After performing in some shows at The Gulbenkian, I fancied myself as the next Alan Bates: so what did I do? I became a teacher.

This is where I get confused sometimes, about life I mean. There are so many roads you can take and most of the time you really wish you had a map. Somehow, growing up, you get the feeling that it will all be much clearer when you turn the next corner or go over the next brow. It just doesn't happen that way.

Yeah, sometimes the fog clears and it's a sunny day but it often turns colder or the way gets muddier. The next bend in the road is far off and when an interesting track leads off to the left or right, you take it; let's go on another adventure. Whoopee!

I think that's why I constantly crave for a companion, someone to chat with and keep me going on the long slog; someone to skip along the bright and breezy lanes with when life is good. But therein lays the rub. All that comes with attachment, responsibility and, dare I say the word, commitment.

How can we know who to trust? Does anyone we meet on our journey have any better ideas about where we're going? Are we even going to the same place? The truth (as I see it) is: I don't really know, so what should I do?

Do I wait for some divine inspiration? Some people commit themselves to following a higher, unseen power and seek for spiritual guidance but not me. In my book, seeing is believing. I let my fingers do the walking, so to speak. The taste of a good pint, the smell of a hot curry or the sound of music in my ears, these are the easily attainable sustainers of my existence. Greater than any of these things though are the delectable curves of a desirable woman and the joy of caressing them.

So, when Liz came into my life, my cup over-floweth. Gone were all my angst ridden thoughts of how I'd ended up in the Lake District and pondering my next turn of fortune. I no longer needed any plans and even my financial situation could take a back seat. I was in love and everything was gonna be just fine. So, I expect you might be wondering how I got up to the Lake District?

Well, like I said, I stayed on in Canterbury as an English teacher. It was a good school with a history of success and kids that wanted, for the most part, to make something of their lives. Seeing them grow up and mature in to young adults gave me a real buzz. Meeting their folks on parent's evenings was a joy for eighty five percent of my lot and as the years passed by I felt I was being assimilated into my environment. I never know whether to welcome this or resist it. My comfort seemed to make me uncomfortable. Almost imperceptibly, the paperwork and the repetition of the terms began to make me restless. At first I shrugged it off but I couldn't dislodge the nasty fear that it just wasn't fair on the pupils in my care.

Then, something very predictable happened. I turned thirty. I went on a bit of a bender, toasting the departure of the last decade with so much alcohol that it was hard to focus on the years that were looming ahead of me. One outstanding thing that came out of my excessive partying was a new relationship; a pucker, deep and meaningful affair with thoughts of settling down, having babies and everything. It was a plan: a huge and scary one. Not unreasonably, I like to try before I buy, so Julia moved in during the summer holiday. That was nearly three years ago.

I believed that I loved Julia. I thought my career was worthwhile and life couldn't get much better but ... but what? There were things I wanted to do that I couldn't name exactly, they just weren't things that seemed possible if I was married and serious about spending the rest of my days in academia. The arguments started and the grass on the other side of the fence was looking very lush indeed. Julia moved out at Easter and I gave notice that I wouldn't be staying on for the new school year. I knew that I had a whole term to come up with something. Guilt was a big problem and I knew deep down that hanging around Kent, or should I say Julia, was very low on my list of preferences.

Much to my amazement, I struck on a solution within a few days. As summer was approaching my mind was beginning to drift towards the pleasures of getting out on the water again. One reassuringly warm and sunny morning in late April, when the bluebells were bedecking the floors of isolated woodland, I absentmindedly strolled into WH Smiths and bought a copy of Sailing Today to fuel my fantasies. Flicking through the back pages I found an escape route via a request for instructors at a place on Lake Windermere.

Three months later, there was I, living life in the slow lane and loving every minute of it. People of all shapes and sizes - but mostly quite affluent - passed through, taking their first steps on a path that, I hoped, would see them share in my love for messing about in boats. Just as I was settling down to the routine of sailing, walking, eating, drinking and sleeping a new activity entered my world ... romancing. After our first day out on the lake, I knew that I never wanted the end of this particular week to come. I wanted Liz there with me, not back in her regular life down in Sussex.

Imagine my joy then, on the Saturday evening before her departure, looking out at the sunset on the far side of the lake, when she agreed to stay on.

What had begun as a holiday romance soon became an

abandonment of self restraint and my free expression of lust-filled joy at being with her in the beautiful environment that we inhabited. Liz, I discovered, had a similar aquatic fixation to me but her preference was for underwater activities and she soon made a name for herself as a diving instructor. As the summer evenings grew inevitably shorter and trade trickled away my fears grew that Liz was hatching a plan to move on. When she told me that she was going back down south, I wept. In her arms, like a child that has just grazed his knee and needs mummy to kiss it better, I wept. I think she understood but she still went.

She had told me that her parents were very well off and that she could do anything that she wanted, within reason. The summer had given her the idea of opening a shop back home selling surfing and diving equipment. She wanted to build up a chain and maybe diversify into organised holidays and all kinds of stuff.

I don't really know why, she didn't say as much, but I felt that I just wasn't part of this entrepreneurial thrust. She didn't ask me and I was too scared of rejection to raise the issue myself. It was a very fond farewell; we agreed to keep in touch. The following week was hell. All beauty had drained away down the M6 in her wake. There needed a change to take my mind off her so I gave in my notice and got a job as a barman.

Having more free time during the day, I set to exploring the hills and going further afield as the autumn colours augmented the magnificence of the peaks, soothing my troubled mind. My phone calls to Liz dwindled away when I heard the news of a new man in her life which, I later discovered, turned out to be Matt. It was a long and lonely winter despite the good humour of the pub regulars and being part of the close community. My New Year resolution was to make yet another fresh start.

Liz was pleased to get the letter that I sent on a bleak January afternoon. The months apart had left me with a fondness for her but no hard feelings. I told myself that it would be a positive step to go somewhere that I had a friend. I don't think I had a choice, I couldn't let it go.

Chapter 2

A week later; it's Sunday afternoon and I have another visitor, Abi. My lovely work colleague has come to check out my pad. I say lovely because she's loving and loveable … but a bit too naïve for my tastes.

After a quick tour and a genuine expression of approval the conversation drifts into the previous evenings activities. It had been a glorious evening, heavy with the promise of summertime. It turns out that we had both gone into town to make the most of it.

"I was in the mingling in with the crowd outside Wests when I saw you but realised you hadn't seen me." Abi informs me.
"Really …? You should have followed me in."
"I would have but we had just about finished our drinks and were about to head off to a restaurant. Maybe you could join us next time?"
"I'd like that. Anyone I know?"
"Not yet …"
There is a pregnant pause as I wait for Abi to elucidate.
"I haven't known him long myself."
My mind goes into 'Inspector Roberts of the yard' mode and the questions have started stacking up already. My curiosity has been engaged and I stare at Abi with a knowing smile that begs the question …. "just good friends?"
Abi doesn't rise to it but does tell me that his name is Tom and they were introduced about six months ago at a theatre group that she helps out with in her spare time. She thinks they have a lot in common.

Abi asks if I'd be interested in helping. I have two options here and no time to make a reasoned response so I fall back on an evasive answer.

"Oh, I'm not sure I'd be able to commit to that."

"Tom had said much the same thing before I met him. He's glad he got involved though now and it's voluntary … so you don't have to sign your life away!"

I refuse the bait and turn the conversation into more familiar territory of difficulties at work. When she's finished her tea Abi makes her apologies to be leaving so soon with an explanation that she needs to prepare for the group's meeting later that evening.

An idea comes to mind that will provide an opportunity to unite my two friends and meet the mysterious Tommy, "How do feel about meeting up for a night out with a friend of mine?"
"Yeah, that would be great!" She smiles back at me.
"Ok, I'll see what I can arrange. How are you fixed for Saturday week?" I suggest.
"Should be ok; we can firm up later. See you tomorrow."

I feel nicely relaxed as I watch her car pull away. I can look forward to finding out more about Tom and getting to know Abi a little better. There is also the unquestionable truth that spending time with her is good for my sanity.

Heading back to the front door I give myself a little smile of satisfaction that my weekend in my new surroundings has gone rather well. With my sense of self-worth being on an even keel and no need to panic about anything looming large at work tomorrow, I fall heavily into the sofa and while away the evening at peace with the world.

Thankfully, a new commitment on Tuesdays is a meeting with Abi. I've agreed to facilitate her role as best I can and hope I'll be able to sit in on one of her sessions. I know she appreciates any help she can get and it may lead to the germination of closer ties. I really should think about some extra-curricular activities but one has to draw the line somewhere between public and private life, otherwise the division can erode to a point of no return; my private life is closely guarded.

So the morning slips by in a haze of administrative detail and essential telephone conversations. A short break for a sandwich in the fresh air at lunchtime and off to a couple of appointments before finishing off some paperwork and heading home. The Theatre has been quite noisy with the technicians stripping down the old in readiness for the new and it's best to keep out of the way on days such as these.

The new day dawns with an altogether sunnier disposition. I manage to mingle with some of the staff, to discuss the prospective arrival of a few 'celebs' the next day, over a vodka and orange in our local. As my familiarity with my new surroundings grows I begin to entertain the possibility of forcing my attentions on some of the unsuspecting cast. I am determined not to be a wallflower here and they are people, after all. We're all in this together as far as I can see and, in a very real way, they need us just as much as we need them.

Much to my relief, Abi checks in for our three o'clock appointment. We adjourn to the small theatre for tea and biscuits and a chat about today's objectives. It's nice to feel wanted as I've been frustrated at the lack of engagement with most of my other, for want of a better word, clients.

My role here is to take her ideas and explore ways of transforming them into exercises for the students to do. It helps her to reach an understanding and that makes it easier for her to work effectively, so she says.

The session today is a continuation of the theme from last week, so much of the groundwork has been done. However, we do need to come up with different ways of interacting to make sure there is no feeling of déjà vu. We scribble and blurt out our ideas until Abi is happy that she has enough meaningful material for an enjoyable hour.

At the end of our brainstorming session there's some time to kill before the first of Abi's class arrive; she's keen to find out who I'll be introducing her to on Saturday. I can feel myself warming to Abi and believe that I can trust her sufficiently to open up a little about my private life.

Time is tight so I gloss over the emotional turmoil that I have endured and stick to the facts. She listens while I eulogise about Liz and what a great time we had on Windermere; I emphasis the beauty and autumnal peace of the fells before explaining the reason for my move following my winter of discontent. Abi makes the link between this Liz and the person that I was staying with upon my arrival. I want to offload on her about more recent events but some students amble in, chatting amongst themselves, and break the bubble of our intimacy.

I see the freshness in their faces and sense something about them that suggests this means more to them than playing pool and drinking Bud.

After some preamble Abi's looking at me way too much for my liking; she continues, "… you've all become aware, I hope, that this afternoon's proceedings are becoming a team effort and I want you all to welcome Andy to our group. Most of you will have heard of him through his involvement with the Theatre and he's kindly agreed to come along and join us today."

With a look and a pause from Abi, I feel the need to say something, off the top of my head, "Erm ... well, it's er ... good to, er ... be here."

These young, inexperienced hopefuls are looking at me with respect and gratitude which suddenly gives me the inspiration to form a coherent sentence.

"It's not often that I get to do anything so hands on and you have a great opportunity in these sessions with Abi. If I can help you along the way and maybe discover some hidden talents then who knows what might happen."

There are smiles on faces and a couple of the older ones come over to shake my hand and are genuinely grateful for in my interest in them. Abi starts with a younger group: getting them talking about developing some ideas while the others spontaneously pick up where they had left things last week. Their time together may be brief but the importance of it is clear to them. Those who have confidence guide the newer or younger members towards relinquishing the struggles of their teenage world. I leave Abi and her cohorts to finish their session; it's a shock to the system when I step out into the noise of the ring road in the rush hour.

I turn my thoughts towards where to go with Abi for our night on the town. After our intimate conversation, I'm feeling something approaching guilt having told so much to a relative stranger. That said, I'm sure Abi will be cool about it. To help me put the nagging doubts to rest, I resolve to ring Liz and broach the idea of the three of us meeting up at the weekend.

Better still, I'll arrange to hook up with Matt and Liz this weekend: show some brotherly love, make up for my recent faux pas and catch up with what's happening in their world.

Yeah.

And have a few beers while I'm at it. Sorted!

Chapter 3

I've gotten to know my way around the city but I'm still glad that our meeting point on this Friday evening is very near the cathedral. There is always a fair few souls wandering the streets in a place of this size. So many people looking for a place to be
and here I am, hungry to join the throng.

Liz will be my guide on tonight's journey of discovery, as she has been since we met last summer. That was a beautiful place to be; I went there to broaden my horizons but I think I may need to change my viewpoint from here rather than just see more of the world.

The awkwardness of a single bloke looking at his watch as if he's been stood up is something I am keen to avoid, so I am deliberately fifteen minutes late at Wests Bar. There is a crowd taking advantage of the last warmth from the sunset and I catch conversations about cars and cricket as I push through the closely packed people in pursuit of Liz or a long cool drink: the drink comes in first. I glance around as the barman pours my drug of choice.

My pulse drops a few beats per minute as I see Liz approaching from a dark corner where half a dozen faces are turning in my direction. I learn that these are our co-conspirators for the fun and games that are loosely planned and will, no doubt, lead back to someone's gaff for a nightcap when the bars have all closed up for another night. Another night that is repeated hundreds, if not thousands, of times every weekend across the length and breadth of small town England.

Matt is the main focus of my attention as I allow the alcohol accumulating in my bloodstream to mellow me out. There is little that one can do to stop first impressions being made but with age comes the added wisdom of books and covers. A joy of living that I'm very familiar with embraces me as the evening passes. After another round, the majority decision is to take a short walk and find some more willing recruits in the Dolphin and Anchor.

My will power dissolved in the warm comfort of my fifth pint. It was fast approaching eleven and I felt sure that I could stay the pace for another hour or two if I continued drinking at the same rate; an illusion reinforced by the acquiescence of my newly found friends and my ability to be increasingly amused and amusing with every flash of a smile. The benefits of previous experiences of inebriation are dredged up from the pit of my stomach as I'm encouraged to drink up before we move on.

I hear myself muttering to Liz "I've had a great time, must do it again soon."
She tries to persuade me to come back to Matt's with her and a couple of the others. I'm trying to grip onto her arm for stability as I make excuses about not being used to the pace and not wanting to have to find my way back in the early hours.

Thankfully, Matt is fairly well gone too and is anxious to get moving so we join in the embrace peculiar to the closing time of night. Once around the corner and heading in the right direction, I inhale the cool air and look up at the stars so as not to worry too much about my feet. As I reach my front door I'm aware of a sense of satisfaction that lasts through the making of coffee and the preparations for bed. The conscious effort of staying awake is willingly dispensed with.

At four o'clock in the morning I need some water, lots of water. At six I head for the bathroom and take on more water with a couple of paracetamol. At eight all thoughts of a relaxed morning are dispelled by the reality of a thumping headache. It's payback time. All actions have consequences and this is a well rehearsed procedure that should have no lasting repercussions. My body just has to accept the lie that my brain tells my soul about alcohol and do its best under the circumstances.

Stage one on the road to recovery consists of a couple of rounds of toast and hot tea with plenty of sugar. According to the *directions for use*, stage two (more paracetamol) cannot be employed for another half an hour so I crawl back into bed and start to wonder what the others got up to after my departure.

But there is no rest for the wicked; I can't get back to sleep with the sun shining in and the sound of happy birds mocking me. Stumbling into the bathroom I down the tablets with another glass of water and catch my reflection in the mirror.
"What you lookin' at?" I scowl at my outer self.
Is it guilt or a sense of my own stupidity that makes me turn away and head back to the relative comfort and security of a soft bed? Either way, oblivion is the desired way out and I feel relieved when I awake in a better state.

After a strong black coffee and a reviving shower, my 'id' is up to venturing into the streets, under the protection of a pair of Raeburns, desiring to procure a Sunday paper and return to base for an afternoon of R&R.

There is a choice to be made between reading the paper and switching on the telly, with the added complication of whether to have a hot or cold drink. There are nine possible options here if you include the one, on both decisions, of doing neither. Obviously the easiest decision is to do neither but it doesn't appeal greatly as I'm not tired enough for option ten.

Twenty five minute pass.

Sorry, what was I saying? I must have dozed off, there.

I definitely need a cup of tea now and I think I can manage a detour via the TV to switch that on, but God only knows where the remote is.

By the time the kettle has boiled, I've located the slob-box down the side of the armchair and flicked through the channels.

Late Sunday afternoon is a real graveyard for television watchers unless you enjoy *The Antiques Roadshow* and *Songs of Praise*. Personally, I don't but I do have enough will power to turn it off and grab the paper on the way back to the lounge with my cuppa.

I'm a bit of a Guardian reader. OK, I know that a high percentage of you will have instantly thought "bloody lefty" or "intellectual dullard" but like many other things in life, you make a decision when you are still too young to know what's what; then you get too old to change and some old habits die hard! Anyhow, today I bought the Mail on Sunday. I've lost the rest of you now, right, but it's easier to read and on a Sunday, I want EASY.

You'd best amuse yourself for a while now; I'm not going to read it to you.

A minute passes.

I made the mistake of looking at the TV page to see what was on later and work out how long I could read the paper for; became very concerned about the potential futility of my evening. Now I'm panicking because I have an option deficiency and the best I can come up with is reading a book.

OK. Plan B. It's too late to think of arranging anything, even if I did have a magic wand to conjure up some new friends or transport me back to the East coast to see my old ones. Hold that thought though; I must do something about arranging a weekend trip home: I phone my mum.

In the knowledge that one day I will be elsewhere, wishing I was with the people that I have yet to meet here; I content myself with passing a pleasant evening in the company of a famous film star; Scarlett Johansson would be my first choice but she is unavailable so I browse through the usual suspects and plump for Kevin Spacey in American Beauty.

Grabbing a large packet of popcorn and a couple of bottles of beer from the kitchen completes the potential harmony of my existence for the next two to three hours. I even decide to silence my phone and enjoy the darkness as the light outside fades to grey.

Lost in the magnificence of the illusion, it is tempting to leave the ordinariness of one's two up, two down life and believe that this new world is reality. Shocking then, especially with such a film as this, when the credits roll, the music plays and the lights go on. I particularly like disturbing films, probably because they take me out of my comfort zone and shake things up a bit in my mind. That's another good reason for doing my current line of work too; there's never a dull moment.

For me, variety is the spice of life and for a brief moment my thoughts return to the promise, if that's what it was, to go to Abi's meeting next week. One half of me is an adventurer who wants to experience those exotic places and events that fate places in my path; the other is afraid that one day I might look under a stone that I should have left unturned.

Being involved with the Theatre has made me realise how much of a performance much of the rest of life is, if you can be bothered to watch the show. In a kind of voyeuristic way, I'm quite looking forward to doing a bit of people watching.

Refreshed by my day of busily doing nothing, there's another manic Monday to be faced. Like Sir Bob, I don't like Mondays. I'm glad that the picture of me which you may have in your head is limited to the amount of information that I give you because, quite frankly, I scare myself when I look in a mirror at 7:30am. It used to worry me, when Julia was so concerned about my appearance and building our little love nest; she drove me mad sometimes.

Anyway, my life is much simpler and uncluttered by such worries today and it's a case of mind over matter, I think. Maybe it's a case of what the eye doesn't see, the heart doesn't grieve over. Whatever, you're sensible enough to work it out for yourself, I hope.

The morning ritual is probably boringly similar to yours unless you're something like a postman or an early morning jogger. Mine is coffee, cereal, shower, teeth, deodorant, dress and go. Maybe one day I will wake with the sound of children getting ready for school and all that that brings. For now though, it's get out of bed as late as feasibly possible and then panic to leave the house before I should be arriving at work.

Television plays a transitory role in of all this, which I have yet to find a pattern for. It's unlikely that there is one, any more than there is in the weather. As the years stack up the inevitable gravitation towards the normality and comforting reliability of the BBC starts to bite. Isn't news a wonderful thing? At least, until you can't take any more of the pain and suffering that surrounds us all and you reach for the off button. Shut it out for a while until your own comfort zone fools you into believing it may be safe to switch back on again.

Blimey, it must be Monday if I'm feeling that cynical; it's time to get my head back into the process of earning a living for five more days. I don't have the right to complain when I think of how good it is to work at the Theatre and they are a good bunch to spend the day with and be creative. I've not been there long enough to get to know everyone, unlike some of them who have been there for decades.

Amazingly, my timekeeping is better than it has been for several months and I should be getting to work in reasonable shape. I doubt that I will be the first in but, if I put my mind to it, I'll have enough time to organise my week before anyone starts beating a path to my door.

One thing that made me feel inclined to accept the post was the thought of being a departmental head. For a while the feeling of maturity and responsibility gave me a bit of a buzz. This declined when I came to terms with the fact that, to all intents and purposes, I AM the department. The upside is that I have little or no requirement to make decisions for anyone but myself and that means I can concentrate one hundred percent on getting things moving.

This has been quite a challenge for me for three very good reasons. First and foremost, my predecessor had already left by the time I arrived, ensuring that there was no handover period for me to pick up where she had left off. Secondly, I am new to the area so there is a lot of fact finding and advice seeking to be done before I start anything. Last and certainly not least, as I think you may have realised, I haven't really done this before.

My team, as I call my growing collection of assorted allies, has been a God send so far and I have already begun to go home on some evenings with a definite sense of achievement.

So, here we are, a short stroll through the pedestrian underpass and across the car park to the unmistakable and, dare I say it, renown architectural features of the theatre.

I make my way around the back, away from the public entrance, to the administration block and on through the reception with a nod to the early starters. The positive vibe about the place which regularly puts everyone on their toes is absent today. Mondays are often the day after the night before when a show has just ended and it's more than likely that many are tired and even saddened by the thought that something wonderful has run its course. Occasionally, as the years roll by, an actor may have become a close friend but for most they are only glimpsed for a few days until another show comes to town.

For me, so far, these undulations have yet to affect my day to day existence. One of my long term goals is to gain the support of some B list actors from the locale to generate some genuine excitement amongst my protégés: thus laying the foundations to attract some bigger names in the future. Indeed, aside from the regular weekly commitments and some rapid bridge building amongst the wider arena of potential players, it is my intention to produce a list of hopefuls by the end of the week.

And so, another working week passes and I'm starting to believe that I have overcome the feeling of unfamiliarity in my new surroundings. By Saturday, I am up for pressing on and furthering my aspirations of being a bit of a party animal. So, at eight o'clock it's time to wander into the city for my rendezvous. I hope that tonight's encounter will lead to many more with the added extra of my own romantic involvement to alleviate a perverse need to take such an unhealthy interest in other people's.

While lost in the ether of the singing birds and buzzing bees I become struck with the wonderful expanse of foliage around me. I remember the previous weekend's conversation with Matt but now, as I walk alone, I become intrigued by the variety and beauty of the vista on display.

My day-dream is shattered by the return of the traffic and I swing into East Street and head for ASK. With time to kill I browse the shop fronts and I'm pleased to see that Abi is loitering outside Next.

When she sees me approach she smiles, ambles over to meet me and says, "Hi, I'm glad you're early too."
"Yeah, I just thought I'd stroll for a while and make sure I was here first to introduce the two of you."
"Well, that's very thoughtful of you, have you had a good day?" She asks.
"Nothing too spectacular; I caught up with myself, so to speak. Phoned my mum and an old friend from university; I might take a trip back home soon. How about you?"
Abi frowns and replies, "Um, so-so. I had to go and talk to one of the group's parents about something; I've been really looking forward to this evening though."
We amble the short distance down to the restaurant.
"Shall we go and wait for Liz inside?" I suggest.
"Good idea. How are you settling in to our seething metropolis?" Abi enquires.
"It makes a nice change from the Lake District."
"In a good way?" She wants to know.
The waiter shows us to our table, giving me time to analyse my own feelings about the place that I have started to call my home, before telling her, "Too soon to say for sure but I have no complaints so far"
"That's good to hear." Abi replies with real warmth.
"Ah, there's Liz."

We exchange looks of recognition and Liz directs the attentive waiter's gaze in our direction.
Liz is obviously on a high this evening. She pecks me on the cheek as she greets me and takes her seat. She smiles at Abi too and introduces herself before I can even begin to speak. I think this puts Abi at her ease and the two of them seem almost oblivious to my presence for a while. We are studying the dessert menu by the time

our conversation flags.

There are a couple of subjects that I have had in mind to introduce at some point in the proceedings and now that the first bottle of wine is empty I seize the opportunity to ask Abi how Tom is.

"Pretty good, as far as I can tell; he's looking forward to meeting you." She says with real sincerity.
"The feeling's mutual."
"Why not come over for lunch with us tomorrow?" She offers.

Liz looks a little confused and Abi explains.
 "Tom's a really sweet guy who started helping out at a youth group that I've been involved with for a couple of years. We've been spending more and more time together lately."
Liz grins and says, "That must have been a real chore, spending all that time with a nice single guy?"

For the first time I see a hint of embarrassment burning into Abi's cheeks and she smiles.
Liz is keen to replenish her empty glass and is scouring the tables for the nearest waiter to instruct in the fulfilment of her desire.

"It wasn't all hard work." Giggling and relaxed, Abi transforms herself in my mind from amiable companion to long term friend in a single, immutable moment.
Liz continues her interrogation, "What's the real attraction then?"

I feel the hint of doubt hit Abi as a look of seriousness sweeps across her face. Liz is distracted from her obsession with the acquisition of more wine and hangs on Abi's response, as do I.

Abi looks skyward as she thinks of Tom and says, "That sort of little boy lost look, I suppose."
Half mockingly, Liz says, "And now he's found, I suppose?"

Liz frowns at her in a way that I might once have replicated, but something makes me hold my thoughts in neutral before deciding upon my response.

As Abi continues to expand on the sweetness and light that has entered her life in bodily form, Liz's attention span seems to have reached its nadir. I begin to wonder whether this wholesome conversation is too deep for Liz. The arrival of the next bottle gives her the excuse she has been looking for to go off on a more familiar road.
"Let's get through this bottle and then make for somewhere more lively … see if there's anyone throwing a party tonight; I could do with some serious night life."
My immediate reaction is that it will, more than likely, prove to be a cul-de-sac.

After another half an hour of listening to Liz's tales of the unexpected and watching her slip down three more glasses in the time it takes Abi and me to finish one, we settle up, fore-going coffees.

As we wander round the corner I try to return to familiar territory by introducing the subject of sailing which I hope will lead to another encounter of a nautical bent. It's an initial success but my plan is thwarted when I see, a few seconds after Liz, a figure in the shadows outside the bar; I recognise her from the previous weekend's session.

She calls out to Liz who returns the greeting and enquires after Matt's whereabouts. For a second or two Abi waits to see whether Liz intends to return and continue their conversation but, when Liz takes the joint that is proffered, we move down the stairwell into the gloom. Neither of us has been beyond the threshold before, although Abi assures me that it is known amongst her friends as, "a decent place for a bit of a boogie". The matter of fact way that she uses this phrase brings a smile to my face.

After a long, hot wait at the bar I joyfully accept the glass which is passed to me and we make for a quieter and cooler corner. Abi seems genuinely concerned for Liz and asks me, "Do you think she'll be alright? She was knocking them back earlier."
I reassure her by saying, "Yeah, no worries. You should have seen her last week … she's just getting started."

As I finish this sentence I realise that I was in an even worse state than Liz and I can't let Abi down by leaving her with a couple of drunks on her hands. Liz's consumption in the restaurant has ensured that I have yet to come anywhere near saturation point. As we are alone and my friend seems to be enjoying our conversation, I place my glass on the table and leave it there while we chat.

Returning to our earlier topic I ask, "What you were saying about Tom, do you think he was a bit lost when you met him? I mean, what brought him here, do you know?"
To which she replies, "We all have some things that we can never say to anyone, not even our own families. I think he was looking for a new start but didn't realise what it was. I hope he does now!"
"Right … maybe I'll ask him sometime."
She encourages my interest by saying, "I'm sure he'd be delighted that you are interested."

Liz stumbles upon us looking much like the proverbial Cheshire cat. Without stopping to listen to what Abi has just said, she puts her arm round her shoulders and asks her if she likes the place.

Abi's response is favourable, "It's a good place to come on a Saturday night. Good music and happy people … can't get much better than that."
Liz, being outlandishly friendly now, says, "Great. If you're ever at a loose end and need to chill out, give me a call and I'll meet you

here. That goes for you too Andy. Not Sundays though, Sunday's a day of rest, right?"

Abi accepts, "You said it. I may well take you up on that. You might even find me in here already; I've a couple of friends who like coming."

"OK. Well, I'm often in here with Matt during the week. We know there'll always be someone in here who is on our wavelength, if you get me." Liz informs us with a wink.

Abi obviously does but declines to follow the lead. I decide to rescue her from the overpoweringly close attention by fishing for the name of the girl in the street. Liz slides over and nestles down next to me. Before long she has moved from the girl's name to a blow by blow description of "her crowd" and their antics. Matt features prominently but there seems to be an element that is being glossed over.

Her tale is enthralling and she is obviously having a fantastic time. Abi and I are both entranced by her joie de vivre but when the story ends she realises that she needs a refill and staggers off to the bar. We decline her generosity by waving a hand over our still half full glasses.

Abi looks at her watch and says that she really needs to think about getting back so that she won't be too tired in the morning. The amplified music seems to have been turned up so I confirm my understanding with a nod. We wait for Liz's return to see what she wants to do next. I start to worry that there is no sign of her propping up the bar.

After a few minutes, checking the details of Abi's invitation the next day and sipping the last mouthful from my glass, I bring her up to speed with Liz's disappearance. Abi, her back to the rest of the room, turns her head to confirm my view.

"I'm just going to look around for her and say goodbye. Meet you outside in a minute?"
"Sure. Say goodbye from me too." She requests.
"Will do. I'm sure she'll be fine … maybe Matt'll be by later …"
"Maybe." She acknowledges as she heads for the door.

Not surprisingly, Liz has met up again with Judy, the mystery girl she encountered outside, who is now very much inside. They seem to be making plans for later so I forgo the unnecessary formality of ascertaining her wishes. She's a big girl.

"We're off now, Liz. Good to see you. Catch you next week sometime, yeah?"
"Definitely." She agrees.
"Abi says goodbye."
"Sorry Andy, hope I didn't upset her. I just need to let my hair down a bit tonight."
"Don't worry about it. She's had a good time." I say, reassuringly.
"Oh good. Have a good time tomorrow." She says and kisses me in farewell.
 "See you around. Bye Judy."
"Ciao."

I leave Liz to her night time experiences, whatever they might entail. I'm content to rejoin Abi in the cool night air and amble down the alley into the main street.

Sadly, I say, "Looks like it's time to go our separate ways …"
"Thanks for a really good evening, Andy."
"I'd love to try some other places out; there seems to be loads to choose from."
Abi, her hospitality never ceasing, says, "Sure … and I know you'd like the country pubs too. In fact, if you like, you could come out on Tom's boat next weekend. We often use it to relax on Saturdays when the weather is nice. We could have some lunch out in the

estuary or stop off at the pub on the way back.

In truth I reply, "Sounds fabulous."

"We'll sort out the details with Tom tomorrow. You haven't forgotten, have you?"

Abi laughs, in the certain knowledge that I haven't.

"I promise to set my alarm as soon as I get in, just in case."

Abi hugs me before she turns away. A few steps later she looks round and waves. I am still standing watching her walk away. A shout from up the street brings me to the realisation that I have been lost in my thoughts again.

For the second week in succession I find myself walking up North Street alone and wishing I had a female companion to share the night air with. This time, however, I am sober enough to feel the discomfort of the situation. I diffuse my pangs of hunger by concentrating on and anticipating the enjoyment of the day ahead.

To my surprise, by the time I turn the key in my front door, the prospect of meeting Abi again has completely submerged the initial regret of leaving Liz to party the night away. But then again, I've been drinking, so pay no attention to anything I say right now.

Goodnight.

Chapter 4

The Cathedral bells awaken me the following morning. I'm already feeling thankful for Abi's influence over my natural instincts to drink myself silly. Man, those bells are loud!

No need for painkillers today though. Just pop the kettle on, select Radio 2 for *Sunday Love Songs,* and take advantage of the time to shake off my sleepy head with a nice cup of tea in bed. Inevitably, after a couple of love songs, I'm starting to wish that I had Liz lying next to me.

Gulping down the last mouthful of lukewarm tea, I burst into action. It's the only way to break my chain of thought. First things first, I switch off the radio. Then, I head for the shower. Once I'm under the luxurious spray, powering from above, I can't prevent myself from assessing my current situation as I cleanse my body.

How long have I been here? Only four weeks! The last two have been a bit of an eye-opener, that's for sure. But I'm feeling that I only have half the picture. One eye is still firmly shut, me thinks. To get things in perspective, I'm going to have to spend some time with my two best mates' other halves and see what floats their boats.

Liz's combustive elements are no secret to me. Let's not dwell on them for too long, eh? Abi though, she's a real surprise package. Do I feel jealous of Tom? No. But I am keen to find out just exactly what it is that Abi sees in him: maybe I could learn a thing or two along the way. As for young Matt, well, I know exactly why Liz would want to hang around with him. What worries me is what will crawl out when I turn over a few stones. I just hope there won't be anything that bites too hard.

Refreshed, dressed and nourished, I do what many city residents do of a Sunday morning: I head out to one of the many coffee shops.

There was a time, many years ago, when North Street would have been an oasis of calm at this time in the week. There would have been no reason to come here; no retail opportunities, back then. A few holy souls might have been sauntering home from the morning service and a couple of early-bird drinkers may have been loitering before opening time but otherwise, nothing but windblown litter to disturb the stillness.

But today, it is people dodging time. Everyone's zipping about, expecting you to get out of their way, totally oblivious of the multitude around them and searching for the next bargain. Ho-hum, I suppose I'm no different. My personal quest is for a reasonably priced Americano.

As I wend my way towards my destination, I read the huge 'SALE' signs in the store windows. There are thirty, fifty even seventy percent savings on offer. It makes me laugh. Buying anything never saves you a penny. It's all an illusion: buy nothing and save one hundred percent!

That reminds me, I have nothing … in my wallet … so I head off to get some *Free Cash*, as the enticement above the dispenser proclaims. I wish.

Another thing I wish for is for some company. I'm happy to sit and drink my coffee alone, while I take advantage of the free newspapers on offer, but it's always nice to have a good natter. I find that it makes me feel more a part of what's going on around me and less like a *Johnny No Mates*. Who shall I ring?

During my reflections early this morning, I had wondered what had been happening with Liz's court appearance and getting Matt to drop by would give me the perfect opportunity to let him unburden himself. With a bit of luck, he might even bring Liz along too.

I pull in to a quiet alleyway, away from the throng, to select his name from my contacts. He picks up.

"Hi, it's Andy."

"'ang on, give us a mo." Matt whispers, obviously moving to another room to talk.

I hang on.

"Ok. What can I do you for mate?"

"I'm just heading into Starbucks; wondered if you were inclined to join me."

"Er … what time is it?"

"It's getting on for eleven thirty." I advise him as I picture Liz slumbering, naked, in the bed that he has just crawled from.

"Oh, right, yeah, sounds good. Give us half an hour."

He's pressed the red button and put the phone down before I can speak again. I'm already starting to wonder who "us" might be.

So, thirty minutes, but most probably more, to grab a good spot in Starbucks. Hopefully it won't be too busy.

As it turns out, the "us" referred to was just him – although he may have intended otherwise. I'm sure all will be revealed, in due course. Matt acknowledges my presence and raises his hand to enact the drinking from a coffee cup to check whether I need a refill. I reply with a *thumbs up* and he arrives with two large dark brews a few minutes later, for which I thank him.

"My pleasure." He assures me.

"Good night was it?"

"Yeah, top notch, as it goes. Ended up at Thursdays, out by the lakes. You should try it sometime."

Matt grinned at me in a way that communicated his thoughts far better than he could speak them. The idea appealed to me.

"Well, if it gets a recommendation from you, then I'm there."

"Don't go on a Thursday though, coz it ain't open." He cracked. A little disappointed by my failure to reciprocate with more than an amused grin, Matt slumps back in his seat.

"Did Liz enjoy it?"

"Liz ... no, Liz weren't there. I think I've upset her somehow." Matt said and paused for thought before continuing, "If that's the way she wants to play it though, no reason why I can't still have my fun, eh?"

It sounded as if Matt was looking for my approval, but I doubt if he was. More likely, he was just trying to measure me up by my response.

"Absolutely." I simply say and he seems satisfied. If only I had the guts to give him my honest opinion.

The chance to find out more is too good to miss, so I press him on Liz's emotional state, viz-à-viz, the drugs charges.

Matt mumbles in his coffee, "Who knows with that woman?"

"I know she's gonna be pissed off with you, for getting her into trouble with the Police." I boldly tell him without anticipating his reaction.

He suddenly roars, "She really screwed everything up Andy, when she got caught."

Matt seems blissfully unaware that his angry outburst might attract a little attention from those nearby. I smile back at the curious glances in way of apology.

More mumbles follow, "She's bound to land me in it eventually."

"Land you in it?" I think to myself. He thinks that sending his girlfriend off to buy drugs and telling the Police some semblance of the truth constitutes landing him in it.

"And what about the bag man? What if they get to him? Things could get heavy if she doesn't keep quiet." Matt continues with renewed agitation.

Suddenly, I wish I hadn't asked. Deep down though, I've always known that it was serious.

"Let's go out for a fag." I suggest, confident that this isn't the best place to be right now.

None the wiser as to Liz's position I press on, once outside.

"Tell me what you know – not what you think you know."
Matt comes clean, at last, "She won't talk to me about it. Every time I try to help her, she just says she doesn't need my advice. I don't think she realises she could get years inside. She'll be up before the judge before too long and if we're not on the same page then I don't know where this is gonna end."
Matt takes a long drag and slowly blows out the smoke.
I do the same as the difficulty of Liz's predicament sinks in. I need to talk to her, but not for the same reasons as the guy standing in front of me. I feel like punching him in the face, if I'm totally honest.
I grind the butt of my spent Marlboro into the pavement and offer Matt my assistance.
"I need a drink mate, you up for one?" He asks, in way of acknowledgement.
"Now you're talking." I affirm with a joyful smile and we head for the nearest bar.

Half an hour later I am sitting on a bench, enjoying another Marlboro and contemplating my next move. I'm due at Abi's for lunch at one o'clock and was so glad to have a good reason to leave Matt in the pub after downing my first pint.
To summarise, and save you from hearing all the nonsense that that bloke comes out with when he's got an audience, I'm fairly certain that Matt ambitions are going to come to a bad end one day. He thinks he's a face and is on the way to great things but, reading between the lines, I reckon he was banking on Liz to keep him in clover while he built his little empire.

"Never crap on your own doorstep" is one on my rules of thumb in life and it's one that I feel I should enlighten Matt with. Surely, he is going to hurt some people on his way up but I'll be damned if Liz is going to be one of them. The current problem however is undeniably real and potentially irretrievable.

As I stub out the cigarette, I make a mental note not to accept another from Matt, or anyone else for that matter. I don't usually smoke, so why start now? Let's go for a walk down to the Palace Garden to see if I can find some divine inspiration there.

I find my thoughts reflected in the random movement of the fish in the ornamental pond but eventually, as I stare into the water, their slow motion calms me to a point where I can think more objectively. Or maybe it was the effect of the nicotine wearing off. Either way, I continue down the cute manicured pathway to meander amongst a variety of trees – none of which I could put a name to. Even here, the Sunday crowds are filtering in from the shops but I manage to find a little piece of turf to call my own. Laying down flat on my back and looking up at the pale blue sky, I try to recall the peace of being alone in the Lakes. The problem with that is, I wasn't alone in the Lakes; I was with Liz.

So, first things first, I need a plan. No, first of all, I need an exit strategy for Liz. I don't see that she can avoid a conviction for possession – having been caught red handed, as it were. Therefore, the only feasible alternative would be to try to reduce her sentence, maybe even avoid prison altogether. I'm sure her lawyer will talk her through all this but my job or my labour of love, more like, must be to bring her to the point where she wants to take his advice. I won't be able to argue the case any better than an expert but where he has the *legalese*, I have the advantage of inside information: what's likely to be going on in Liz's mind, that is. It's all a question of whether I still have access and can reach her head via her heart. Getting her to turn against Matt might just look like sour grapes but no, I don't want to make excuses for myself; I want to land him in it.

If I can get her to see that Matt is expendable then maybe the Police will believe that she was just a go-between, when she names the guilty parties whom she was merely aiding and abetting. Assuming that she wasn't drink driving or high then her lack of previous might just swing it for her. Ok, it's not going to be easy but I can't just sit back and watch.

Anyway, all that will just have to wait for now. I need to get moving if I'm going to be on time. I need to pick up a bottle of wine on the way. Oh, maybe some mints to stop my breathe smelling of fags and booze would be a good move too.

Here goes for a little adventure to find an address out on the east side of the city. It's not far and her hurriedly drawn map on an office notelet brings me to Abi's door just a few minutes late. The prospect of spending the afternoon with Abi … and Tom … gives me a surprisingly relaxed attitude; I have a real feeling of optimism that has somehow alluded me in my efforts to rebuild old bridges.

After the door bell sounds, I faintly hear Abi calling, "Can you get that Tom?"
There is a pause that gives me time to put on a happy smiley face to greet the man as he pulls back the shiny expanse of white UPVC that separates us.
"Hello Andy, come on in."
Complying with his request, I hand Tom the bottle and tell him it's my small contribution to help the food go down.
He checks the label and thanks me, with genuine happiness written on his face. I follow him into the lounge whereupon he takes my gift into the kitchen.
Abi appears in his stead, resplendent in a classic blue and white striped chef's apron.
"Good to see you Andy", she affirms as she kisses me on the cheek.
"Make yourself at home."
"Thanks."
I take in the décor and the seating options and settle into the comfy single seat with a view of the wide arch that leads to the kitchen, through which Abi has now been replaced by Tom; he struggles to open the bottle of wine but manages to remove the cork while we

continue to exchange pleasantries. He puts the bottle on the already laid dining table before falling into the three-seater sofa adjacent to me.

"Lunch won't be long; just waiting for the roasties to brown off. Are you hungry?" he enquires.

"I am now that I can smell what's cooking. I always enjoy a good roast."

"Ah, you're in for a treat then … Abi's cooking is the best."

Abi hears the praise and calls out from behind the wall, "Flattery will get you nowhere Thomas!"

Ignoring the put down, Tom elucidates, "I really look forward to coming back here after church on a Sunday, sharing a meal and kicking back for a couple of hours – especially with friends."

Mention of the C word has the effect of reducing my relaxation level a notch or two but figure I'll just let it ride and wonder whether it will be come up again before the dessert course has been completed. Mind you, having had a pint already and with an open bottle of red breathing away nicely, awaiting consumption, who knows what kind of mood I'll be in by the time we get to coffee? A frank exchange of views and a rigourous debate could prove highly entertaining!

The one thing I do know about my host is that he has a boat, so that seems like the perfect subject to start on to get me back in my comfort zone. I'm soon enthralled by Tom's description of his modest vessel moored in the local Marina and how he and Abi had navigated their way around the Isle of Wight in the Spring. Before long though, he's asking me about my previous experiences out on the water and we begin to compare the respective dangers of the North Sea and the English Channel, in a compulsively engaging way.

By the time Abi interrupts our banter with a cheery, "Grubs up!" I have already come to the conclusion that I like this guy.

Settling myself in at the dining table, I half expect one or other of them to say grace but they just start passing dishes of steaming vegetables around with an invitation to help myself. My glass is filled with the red wine, which I take a large swig from before I tuck in. Abi checks my progress and pronounces a semi-formal welcome and we all chink glasses.

"Were you two talking about boats?" Abi asks and gets the nautical conversation back on track.
"Yeah, Andy's going to be a good man to know when we want to go out of the harbour."
"Oooh, high praise indeed Andy." Abi smiles at me in support of her admiration.
"Well, it would be great to get out there and get some practice in. It'll be my first time out on a boat the size of yours for quite a while."
"Ah, I'm sure it will all come flooding back in no time." Tom predicts, confidently.
"We'll see. When are you thinking of taking her out again?" I'm keen to know.
"Well …"
And so our excellent afternoon goes on … and on … and on until, eventually, we get to coffee. The wine bottle was empty and I was stuffed. Was it the drink? Could it have been the generous way in which these two *luv-ly peo-ple* had invited me out to do some sailing or was it a genuine interest? I can't honestly tell you, but I hear myself agreeing to come with them to their evening meeting next week – when I am sober!

With the caffeine from the black coffee working through my veins, I set about helping Tom clear everything from the table and firing up the dishwasher, while Abi takes a well earned break in the garden.

"All done." Tom happily informed her as he stands behind her and gently massages her shoulders.
Ah, nice, I thought as I join them and take in the vista of Abi's small

but well maintained garden.

Then, a second thought came to me. These people had had little or no time to themselves all day and it is probably a good time to be on my way.

"No, really, I think I need to walk off all that wonderful food or I'm likely to fall asleep in the chair." I insist, to negate their protestations.

"Falling asleep is good." Tom counters.

But he senses my need and Abi gets up to give me a truly friendly hug before I make my way to the front door.

Tom shakes my hand and tells me that he's very glad to have got to know me today.

"Likewise."

The door softly closes and I make my way up the street, enjoying the warm sunshine on my face. As I amble along, in no hurry at all and with no concern for the challenges of tomorrow morning, all I can think of is the Bank Holiday weekend to come and the chance to be out on a boat again.

Even though the evening is spent on my own and I torture myself with the on-going dilemma of whether or not to initiate a difficult conversation with Liz, my blissful state of mind lasts well into the following week. I hear nothing from her, so I let it ride. How long I can leave it? Until Thursday, is the answer. I decide to text her to ask if she has any news about her court date, hoping that she will be forthcoming about what's been going on in her life since I left her in the bar on Saturday night. Four weeks seems a seriously long time for Liz to await her fate ... unless she is hiding something from me.

On Friday, nearly twenty four hours on without a response, I close down my computer at the Theatre and take a stroll down North Street, past the Market Cross and into South Street. Confused by Liz's silence, I've decided to do something that I should have done before: check out her new store. I guess if she's ok, she'll be there and we can have a catch up while she closes up. If not, then I might get an update from whoever's running things in her absence. Seems like a plan to me, but I'm still nervous as I reach the excessively watersports orientated shop front.

It's not huge, but none of the shops down this end of town are. The buildings are all so "oldie-worldie" that it's hard to see how you'd get any planning permission for major structural changes. But you've got to start somewhere and there are bound to be bigger and better opportunities further afield once she's made a name for herself, which I have every confidence that she will, if only she can stay out of jail!

Here goes then. Once inside, I scan the walls and feel at ease with the familiarity of the stock on display. It's nicely done and I feel encouraged to browse; no sign of Liz, or any staff for that matter. I wasn't aware of any alarm going off as I opened the door and there are no other shoppers to be seen. I guess that it's the time of day when you have to think about cashing up so maybe I should make my presence known.

I simulate a cough. No response.

The thought of picking up something really expensive and walking out with it enters my head and I scan the corners for CCTV cameras. Even thought there are none, I feel slightly uncomfortable about having had the thought.
My conscience pricking, I speak her name, "Liz, are you there?"
A disconnected head appears from behind a curtain. It doesn't have Liz's face on it.
"Hello," the young woman says, followed by, "can I help you?"
"I was looking for Liz." I tell her, by way of clarification.
"Oh, sorry, you mean the owner ... I'm an Elizabeth too but I'm called Beth in here, to avoid confusion."
"Right, good." My quest is still unresolved.

"She's not here, I'm afraid; hasn't been in all week. Did you place an order?"

"No ... no, it's a personal call."

"Ok, have you tried her at home?"

"Not recently, just thought I'd surprise her."

"Do you want to leave her a message?" Beth asks. "She may be back in tomorrow ... but I don't honestly know myself."

From the way her voice trails off, I guess that she may be hoping for something more from me.

I see an opportunity to fill in some blanks while simultaneously appearing to be a Good Samaritan so I ask, "Do you mind telling me when you last heard from her?

"Not since Monday morning when she said I'd have to look after the shop until further notice ... but she didn't even tell me why. I've had to lock the door just to take a break. It's really not on."

I agree, "No, that's not good."

Beth and I exchange a look of mutual contemplation before I add, "I'm sure there'll be a good reason for it. I'll try and find out where she's got to."

"That would be great. Thanks. Saturdays are always very busy in here and there's no way I'll be able to cope on my own." With a cheeky grin Beth adds, "I don't suppose your free to be my assistant, are you?"

"Unfortunately not, I'm afraid ... otherwise I'd have gladly helped out. I've done some bar work in the past and know quite a bit about all this gear, so I'm sure I'd manage."

"That's a shame. Well ... let me know how you get on with Liz."

I promise to find out what I can ASAP and we swap business cards with personal numbers on the back.

As I leave the shop, I guestimate Beth's age and do the math on the gap. In excess of ten years, I'd say. I suppress my fledgling interest in an more intimate liaison and replace it with a more mature appreciation of her joyful personality. I can see exactly why Liz hired her.

The question is: if she's not answering her phone or going to work then is there any point in visiting her at home? I just can't imagine Liz sitting in the dark and pretending that she's not there. That would just be too odd. Heck, I don't have any plans, so why not? I'll trying calling her one more time, leave a message to say that I'm on my way over for a cup of tea and a chat and just hope that she opens up.

Liz's place isn't far. With her parents' support, she never really does living on a budget. Her flat is more of a luxury apartment and it's close to all the amenities – which basically means that it's expensive. I reckon daddy bought it for her – as an investment, no doubt – so she has no worries about boring stuff like mortgage repayments. You could say that she's a little spoilt but I like to see her as a free spirit. I don't believe that she wants to live her life on handouts; she has ambition and drive aplenty.

My arrival at the curiously named Roman Quarter development, close to the old wall, comes with the sensation, paradoxically, of entering a world of modernity that is centuries apart from the historical ambience of the streets that I have just left. Affluence and dominance are the words that spring to mind in relation to the invaders that constructed the original defences. But hey, it is nice, there's no doubt about that.

Residing here for two weeks before finding my permanent home was not a comfortable experience, despite the luxurious interior space. My confinement to the second bedroom and the need to re-establish a new set of rules for our friendship meant that I had been quite relieved to be packing my meagre belongings and putting a little distance between us, when it came to it. Standing in front of Liz's block reminds me of all this and the reason for my own reticence to make this simple call becomes clear. I press the Call button on the intercom. I press it again a minute later. No surprise. She just isn't there. End of.

Looking around me, an obvious and pleasant explanation jumps out at me - her Dad. Maybe he's taken his little girl back in her hour of need: his only daughter may have flown home. But that doesn't explain why she isn't answering calls on her mobile. Oh, I gotta get off this; it's doing my head in. As promised, I ring Beth - who's still closing up the shop - to let her know that I've got no further and wish her well for tomorrow.

And so I head off along the wall. A stroll across the park and I'm home. It's only an hour since I finished work but I'm drained. After changing into some more casual clothes, I head for the chippie and enjoy eating al fresco back in the park. My mind's made up, I'm going to just enjoy my Bank Holiday weekend and wait for Liz to decide when she wants to contact me. I think three unanswered texts and a voicemail are enough evidence of someone who doesn't want to talk to me right now.

Saturday is superb. I love the month of May and days like these are the reason why. There is a crisp freshness in the air as I open the passenger door of Tom's car in the car park. The sky is a beautiful light shade with a few wispy clouds and the sun begins to warm me as we walk towards the clustered masts in the Marina. The excitement that I can feel through my steadily increasing heart rate also warms me. Abi looks back and smiles at me as we finally turn onto the pontoon where Tom's boat awaits us.

From our conversation the previous weekend, I know what I'm looking for and I spot the distinctive wooden structure on the gaff rigged cutter amongst the shining white Fibreglass hulls of the more commonly acquired vessels. I'm impressed. Tom slips confidently aboard and reaches out to help Abi do likewise. I delay my transition for a moment as I pace the length of the sleek yacht and admire it's craftsmanship and overall beauty.
"Very nice." I simply say with a couple of affirmative nods thrown in.
"Let me show you how well she handles." Tom insists as he beckons

me aboard, eager to caste off.

And off we jolly well go, pootling along to the sound of the outboard until we reach the lock and come to a brief halt as the water levels equalise and the external gates release us.

Once out in open water, Tom and Abi are quickly into action raising the sails and I merely sit back and admire their teamwork for a while.

But Tom has other ideas, "OK Andy, you can take over from Abi now."

We're leaving Chichester Channel to sail out into the wide expanse of the English Channel and I'm relying on Tom to navigate and give me instructions. Abi is down in the cabin checking the charts and brewing up since the sea is fairly calm and progress is smooth. Quite quickly though, I'm beginning to get the impression that I'm working the hardest, moving around the boat as directed and building up a sweat. However, it's all good fun and once again I'm quite relaxed spending time with Tom and Abi.

Abi's head reappears in the doorway to the cabin and three cups are handed on to Tom at the tiller. He sets a straight course of least resistance and the crew gather on deck to just kick back for ten minutes. The sense of space and freedom is just awesome with the added delight of other boats to watch as they glide past on their own adventures into the vast horizon that surrounds us.

Two glorious hours are spent tacking and jibing our way around and trying to make the best of the light wind available. The sun is high overhead as we slip back into the safety of harbour waters again and drop anchor in a relatively secluded spot with a reassuringly attractive view of the coast on our starboard side. There is still a regular flow of larger boats heading out on our port side which Abi and I watch, absent-mindedly, as we talk and listen to Tom whistling below as he prepares our lunch.

"Any word on Liz?" she asks.

"Unfortunately not." I reply with succinct brevity and a wistful stare at a gull riding the breeze a little way off above our mast.

I go on to explain my attempts to contact her and my hope that she might be safely wrapped up on the country estate, oblivious to my feeble emotional turmoil.

She picks up on my self-doubt and tells me, "Don't give yourself a hard time over her Andy; I'm sure you have her best interests at heart. Sometimes all you can do is just love people unconditionally. If she has any sense then she'll see how much you care and then you'll be able to help her."

"I know; you're right. I should stop worrying about it."

"What would you think if I said I could set you up on a date with someone a lot less complicated?"

"And who might that be?" enquires Tom, who is framed by the cabin doorway: his face beaming with the joy of a man who is having a really good day.

"Mel." Abi informs us.

"Ah, Melanie." Tom reiterates. "Well, come on down and have some lunch and you can tell Andy what you're scheming."

The interior of Tom's boat is charming, comfortable and surprisingly spacious. The old phrase "two's company, three's a crowd" would apply well here though. Trying to squeeze another diner in makes for a very cosy arrangement.

The intimacy of the enclosed space only adds to the atmosphere of conspiracy as Abi outlines Melanie's attractive character traits and extols her virtues. Tom nods and occasionally interjects and comes across as quite positive about Abi's plan. His approval is welcomingly reassuring.

I don't say a word; happy to sit, listen and enjoy my lunch.

"And just what have you told Melanie about me?" I wonder.

"Oh, that you're a sad, hopeless case that needs someone to sort you out ... obviously." Abi teases me.

"Really! She's up for that is she?"

"She can't wait; she likes a challenge."

"Excellent. When can I meet her?" Joking aside, I do really want to know.

"Well, you'll get a chance tomorrow, as it happens." Tom is happy to tell me. "More wine?"

"Yes ... thanks." The relief of discovering that I will be casually introduced at their group fills my mind as the sparkling white wine pours into my plastic beaker. I lean back, take a sip and concentrate on the sensation of the cool, sweet fizzy liquid as it quenches my thirst. Lunch is nearly over.

Tom and I discuss returning to the Marina while we finish our drinks and Abi tidies up in preparation for setting sail once more. Soon, the safety of the mooring is in sight and it's time to adjust to life on terra firma for the foreseeable future. Not wishing for the day to end too soon, we take a walk around and check out the coastal view; it's beautiful. Abi enlightens me on the various opportunities available if I wanted to come down and explore the area on foot – including the pub on the shoreline.

Tom drops me back home around three thirty. Not for the first time today, I think of Beth all alone in Liz's shop and, now that I'm alone and buoyed up by my perfect day out on the water, I fetch the card she gave me from my wallet. I ring the number printed on it.

To my amazement, the voice that I hear is not Beth's. It's Liz's. It takes me a couple of seconds to get over the surprise and so there is no prepared response after she completes her spiel and has asked, "... how can I help you?"

"Hello ..." she adds when I don't answer.

"Hi ... Liz ... it's Andy. How's it going?" My brain has re-engaged.

"Oh. Hi. Can I call you back? I can't talk right now."

"Sure. Anytime. It'll be good to catch up." I tell her, in all sincerity.

"Great." She says without sounding great at all; she hangs up.
Short and sweet; I am none the wiser. Patience is required. At least I know that she's back in the land of the living – which is good.
She doesn't ring that evening.
She doesn't ring on Sunday either.

I contemplate the possibility of Mel being as gorgeous as Abi made out and the potential for something altogether less stressful to begin. By the time I close my front door for the extremely short walk – to the other side of the road – I have counted my chickens many times over. But, I have resisted the urge to ring Liz.

The Church Hall looks old on the outside but has a modern interior. Abi has maintained a certain amount of secrecy about her Sunday evening activities except for the fact that is a drama group and great fun. I have no idea what it is, exactly, that I've volunteered for but Tom and Abi seem like really genuine people so, how bad can it be?

Life is full of surprises; it turns out to be a puppet show! Now I am confused. There are voices behind a black curtain. Maybe I should say whispers and giggling. A green headed lady, reminiscent of something from The Muppets, appears and starts to talk to me. You'll just have to imagine the silly voice which sounds vaguely like Abi's.
"Helloo Andrew. Glad you could come along tonight."
I'm uncertain whether to engage in conversation with the puppet or not. I chose not.
Another head appears in a Rastafarian *stylee*. Tom's voice is even sillier.
"Hel-low-dare man. Grea-To seeyoo brudder." Phonetically.
I'm sure another head is about to appear. It does. It's a purple headed lady with long blonde braids. The sexy sounding silly voice comes from an unknown female, presumably Mel.
"Ooh, I'm sooo please to see you Andy. Why don't you come on in and give us a hand?"

A real human hand appears through a split in the side curtain to indicate the way in and I follow the direction into another cosy enclosed space.

I'm introduced to the person with the sexy voice. It is a little dark in there but my first impression is a good one.

"I had no idea you were a puppeteer Abi."

"A girl's got to have some secrets. Shall we retire to the kitchen and grab a coffee?"

"Lead on ..."

As I listen to Abi describe the purpose of the puppet show, Tom sets about brewing up four coffees. I try to concentrate on what Abi is saying about visiting some of the local churches and working with children while at the same time scanning Mel's features under the bright strip light.

At last, Tom arrives with the coffees and I start to feel a little less self-conscious about the whole thing.

"How are you settling in at the theatre?" Mel enquires of me, directly.

"All good, so far; I'm loving it actually. Linking up with Abi has been an added bonus."

"She's a real star, isn't she? I can remember when I first came along to this – wondering what I was doing here – and she just made me feel right at home. Haven't had a single doubt since."

"Stop it, you two ..."

"No, credit where credit's due ..." Tom concedes, "... it's good to get some encouragement for the things you do."

"Well ... thank you ... now drink your coffee!" Abi demands, looking sheepish.

The ice broken, I'm a bit of a spectator as my enthusiastic friends, aka the three amigos, practice their routine for their next show, which is only a week away so time is of the essence. My cover story, for my introduction to Mel, is that I'm a suitable critic for possible improvements. As I sit and perform my duty, with much hilarity, I wonder at a couple of sub-plots that Abi may be hatching. No doubt, Tom would be in on it too. And Mel? Maybe.

I'm sure that my interest in expanding my small repertoire in to puppeteering is being tested. It's obviously a lot of fun and within my capabilities, I would think. But, do I want to get involved. Maybe Mel would be a bit of an enticement. The jury's out on that one.

More subversively, and maybe the stick to go with the carrot, is all that do-goodiness required to help out with a good cause. Am I going to feel guilty about NOT wanting to lend a hand? Or, will the content – Sunday School stuff – make it a no-brainer because, as an *ac-tor*, I have just got to believe in my character, darling!

True to form, I guess, my responses are non-committal but pleasantly appreciative of their work. I recognise the need to big up Mel though and let her know that I have noticed her contribution.

While we're talking, over another coffee in the kitchen, my phone vibrates in my pocket. I pretend not to notice and it goes dead. After a short pause, it gives a shorter repeat performance to let me know that someone has left me a voicemail. I ignore this too but mentally acknowledge the probability that it is from Liz, by a process of deduction: the only other person who is likely to ring my mobile on a Sunday evening is in the room with me.

The evening is drawing to a close and I'm wondering how to tee up a conversation with Mel about meeting up; what one might call a *date*. To my great relief, while Tom and Abi are occupied in some cupboard reorganisation, Mel gets things started.
"Abi tells me you've been sampling the nightlife together."
"We certainly have ... I'm sure there's plenty more to see though ..."
"Have you any plans for next weekend?" She invitingly asks.
"Not yet, but I'm open to suggestions."
I find myself being offered a card with an attractive woman's

telephone number on it for the second time this weekend.
"Give me a ring on Saturday and I may have thought of a couple."
The card reads: Dr Melanie Thorpe BSc Applied Psychology.
"Wow." Is all I can say to that.
"Don't worry, I haven't started analysing you … yet."
Mel has a brief farewell conversation with Abi as Tom continues to mess about in the cupboard. She then whisks past me with an equally casual, "Call me, yeah?"
The door swings to behind her and she's gone.

Tom finally manages to get the cupboard to close and the three of us head out into the cool of the sunset. It feels like a magical evening as the two of them saunter off, hand in hand, leaving me at the top of the steps to the pedestrian underpass. I head off home and check my phone messages as I amble through the tunnel. I was right, it was Liz calling.

Once inside, I throw the phone on the table. I'm not in the mood to ring back; it can wait until tomorrow.

Chapter 5

Hallelujah! It's a Bank Holiday; I don't have to get up and go to the office and I no longer have a huge empty void where my love life is concerned. I do have an important phone call to make though. I play Liz's voicemail to get myself in the zone before I call her back.

I'm feeling attuned, so here goes. After several rings, I get her answer phone message but I hang up rather than leave one. I figure she's either asleep or gone out already. Hopefully she hasn't disappeared again. This thought makes me wonder whether I should have been more willing to try her before I went to bed last night.

I catch myself getting wound up again and give some thought to yesterday evening's highlights. To amuse myself, I try to imagine the girlie chats that Abi and Mel might have had – and even may be having right now – about it all. Somehow, I get the impression that Mel is a very independent woman though and maybe I'm just another in a line of guys that have been given the opportunity to impress and been found wanting. But then again, I can't accept the possibility that Abi would be a party to that. Relax Andy, it'll be fine, I tell myself.

After lunch, with my day slipping away and still waiting on Liz to call, I decide to get some air by taking a stroll across the park in the direction of the Roman Quarter. A quick buzz on her intercom will resolve the issue of her whereabouts, one way or the other.

It's another beautiful day; mid twenties with a light breeze and blue skies. The Priory Cricket Team has been working on their square and the Council grounds men have kept the place looking very neat and tidy. With the centuries old Guildhall as a backdrop, a more unmistakably English setting would be hard to imagine. Not wanting to let the moment pass me by, I find an empty bench to linger on and bask in the sunshine.

In a determinedly good mood, I reach Liz's quarters and press the call button once again but more hopefully, this time around. And my optimism is well founded. Whether she saw me coming or just assumed it would be me, I don't know, but she's buzzed me in before I can say, "Its Andy."
The door has been left open for me to walk straight in and I make my way toward the sound of a boiling kettle. In the kitchen, I find her; she doesn't look great, even through my rose tinted spectacles.

My mind goes back to that night at the Police Station. Maybe now, and only now, has the reality hit home to her. This time however, we are not in an interview room, we're in the safety of her abode and she needs a friend, a really good friend, to give her a consoling hug. I go straight to it and she opens her arms out and holds on to me for a good minute or more before I can feel her relaxing a little.

"We've got a lot of catching up to do." I suggest.
"Yes." She simply replies and turns to blip the kettle.

After completing the process she hands me a mug and I follow her through the open lounge and onto her spacious balcony. Liz looks better with sunglasses on as we chill out for a while.

"Where do I start?" She asks, more to herself than to me, but I answer.
"You could tell me where you've been for the past week; I was worried about you."
"Well ... not long after you went home with your nice friend last week, I freaked out. I think it might have been due to the fact that I couldn't find Matt and you were obviously having a good time."
"But you were having a whale of a time, weren't you?"

"You'd think?" She says and then pauses to look out over the rooftops.

"Anyhow ...", she continues, "I got a bad attack of paranoia when I came round on Sunday, all alone. I just thought that I had to split and get miles away from Chi."

"So, you didn't go to your folks?"

"Not straight away, no. I thought I'd head off to the West Country for a couple of days and see what the surf was like." I can see that the mere memory of it has removed one or two worry lines from her face.

"I didn't want anyone to know where I was, which was probably quite selfish, but I did let Beth know that I was away – well, that much you know. Trouble was, I liked being away so much I couldn't face coming back." A small sigh ensues.

"My phone was ringing so often that I had to turn it off; it was the only way ..."

"The only way to do what?"

"The only way I could get any peace – the thing that I needed most of all."

Liz lights a cigarette and offers me the open packet; I decline with a slight movement of my head. She takes a long drag and folds her arms as if hugging herself for further comfort. I can tell that this isn't at all easy for her; I await her next utterance with a sympathetic gaze and hope that I might get to hold her again before too long.

"I had to turn it back on eventually, of course. I picked up a voicemail from my father ... which was a surprise. I thought I'd be back home well before he'd even notice that I'd gone."

"Had you told him anything about the court case?"

"Good God, no!" She says, accompanied by nervous laughter. "I discovered that one of his Constabulary buddies had had a word."

"Oh no, that's not good."

"Well, actually, it turned out alright." She is clearly pleased to be able to say.

"While we're on the subject, you could bring me up to speed about your bust ..." I suggest.

"Oh, I am really sorry, have you been left out of the loop Andy? I thought Matt would have kept you updated."

"It obviously slipped his mind."

"He's unreliable, to say the least ... but let's not talk about him. Come inside and I'll fill you in; I'm never quite sure who might be listening out here." Liz instructs me as she looks out at the adjacent apartments and adds another butt to the pile in the ashtray.

The lounge is quite minimalist in its decor which adds to the airy feel of the room; the leather sofa which I fall into feels large enough for both of us to lie down on together. There's an empty wine glass on the coffee table which Liz sees and remembers the half empty bottle of white in the fridge.

"We can polish off a bottle of Chablis, if you like."

"I like." I confirm and she slips into the open plan kitchen to retrieve the bottle and a second glass.

Once we're settled and sipping, Liz cracks on with her tale.

"So, what I should have told you last week - and the main reason for getting out of my head - was that I had been to court the day before."

Liz pauses, checking my reaction. I say nothing so she nervously proceeds.

"I wish you'd been there Andy. Matt was so adamant that I should plead not guilty; he was coming up with so many lies for me to tell, I think my lawyer was getting a bit irritated by him. First of all he was trying to get him to believe that the Police had planted it ... which he wasn't having anything to do with. When that didn't play well he suggested that someone I'd given a lift to might have dropped it in there."

"That sounds a bit desperate to me." I interject.

"I think he is desperate; feeling guilty, I expect. I just didn't want to go in to the court hearing without his support but that meant going against my lawyer's advice."

I waited for her to continue as she refilled her glass and drained the rest of the bottle into mine.

"Anyway, the long and the short of it is that I went through with the *Not Guilty* plea, just to buy time. Matt said he'd get a better lawyer sorted out and *we'd* take our chances with a jury. Thing is though, it's *me* that has to pay the price if I lose."
"Absolutely." I readily reply.
"But I would have thought it'd be to his advantage if I pleaded guilty, took what was coming and we could put it behind us."
"Yeah, but once you admit it, it raises some more questions, doesn't it? Like where it came from. Maybe he's getting some grief from some interested party." I suggest.
"What, Simon? He wouldn't do that." She protests.
"No, not even if he was being leaned on?"
Liz takes time to consider the scenario.
"And let's be honest, how well do you think you know Matt?" I throw in.

A heavy silence descends. That was a question that has been on my mind for many days and now it's out there; I've said it.

"Argh!" Liz eventually replies, throwing back her head, as if shouting at the devil.
She then grabs her cigarettes and goes back out on the balcony.
I follow.

"I'm sorry Liz. I shouldn't have asked you that." I backtrack.
"No ... no, there's no need to apologise. That's the real reason I had to get away. It wasn't so much the court that upset me; I had to go somewhere that Matt wasn't, to make my own mind up."

Inwardly, I punch my fist skyward in celebration. Outwardly, I ask, "And what conclusion did you come to?"

But she answers my question with one of her own, "Tell me honestly Andy, has he ever mention a girl named Claire?"

"Only in passing."

"So you've never seen them together?" She probes.

"No, not to my knowledge ... I wouldn't know what she looked like anyway. I can guess where this is going though Liz."

"So you don't think I'm just being paranoid?" She cracks on with question three.

"I'm probably not the best person to ask, am I?"

"Maybe not ..." She agrees, softening her voice and looking into my eyes, "... but you know me better than most, don't you Andy. Just tell me what you think."

"Ok, if I must." I concede but give myself a few seconds to decide where to begin.

"I honestly don't know who this Claire might be. But, I am sure that she was with him on the night you spent in the cells. I can't tell you any more than that and it may have been totally innocent for all I know. He certainly hasn't said anything since then. But, even if you are being paranoid, I'm really worried about where your relationship is leading you."

I leave that simple thought with her before I go too far by gratifying myself with a little character assassination. What's more, I don't want to walk out of here feeling bad about slandering Matt when he's not here to defend himself, however much I believe that I speak the truth.

My self control results in a very positive and pleasurable response. Liz takes a step towards me and hangs her arms around my neck. For a second she meets my gaze and I can see excessive moisture in her tear ducts. A brief thought of planting a kiss on her lips is banished by her resting her head on my chest.

She whispers, "I know. I know. So am I."

After a silent, intimate moment which is all too short from my point of view, Liz removes herself from my embrace and goes back inside to draw a tissue from a box on the coffee table. She had succeeded in holding back her tears but not in smudging her eyeliner. I watch her as she tidies her appearance in the wall mirror and notice her occasional glances at my reflection.

"Look at the state of me." She says as she turns to show me the result of her efforts.
"You look just fine Liz." I reply, with little regard for her make-up malfunction. "Do you want me to go?"
"God, no Andy; not unless you have to."
"No, I've nothing to rush off for. I'd really like to know that you're gonna be ok before I go anywhere, to be honest." I re-assure her.
Liz sits on the edge of the sofa, just about holding it together.
I carry things forward, "So, what's the news with your father?"

"Speaking to him on the phone was a real relief. I can't tell you how much it meant to me to know that he wanted to help me and not disown me. Not that he promised me anything; he just told me to come home and spend the day with him on Sunday, so that we could talk it over. I took some time to prepare myself and travelled up late on Friday; as he was spending all day at his Golf Club on Saturday I thought I'd go in to the shop and do something useful. It wasn't too busy and it was good to get back. Thankfully, apart from you, I don't think anyone found out that I was back and I certainly wasn't going to publicise the fact. So, I was up early and joined my dad for breakfast."
"How did that go?" I asked, hoping for some sort of *Get Out of Jail Free* card that Liz can play, but I am sadly disappointed.

"He was very sure about the best way to deal with the Police but there were some serious drawbacks: not least, having to give up everything I have worked for."

I wait for her to elucidate.

"I just can't see that there is anything I can say in court that will get me off ... so I don't think I have any choice. Dad reckons the Police will question Matt sooner or later and may have some CCTV evidence lined up."

Liz gives me a resigned smile.

"So, I'll just have to come clean and hope that I get off lightly for a first offence. Dad is one hundred percent behind my rehabilitation. I hate the thought of being some sort of Judas though. I won't be able to show my face around here afterwards Andy."

"Well, maybe your best off out of it Liz." I suggest.

My mind has already made the giant leap in my imagination to the two of us returning to the Lake District and picking up where we left off last year. Fortunately, Liz speaks again before my mouth blurts out the idea.

"I'm sorry for dragging you all the way down here and getting you mixed up in all this; it wasn't what I had planned at all."

"Hey, don't you worry yourself about that." I tell her as I put my hand on her knee and lean in to emphasise my sincerity.

To my immense satisfaction, Liz reciprocates by laying her hand on mine.

"This is gonna get a whole lot worse before it gets better, you know?" Liz speculates.

"I don't doubt it ... but you'll come through it."

"And if I lose everything, you'll stick by me?"

"Sure will." I respond to her question which, for me, is a no-brainer.

"Ok, let's do it then." She concludes. Half smiling and half crying, she closes the gap between us and holds me tight to show her appreciation.

However tough it might get, right now I feel it will all be worthwhile.

There's a brief moment as we part when we both seem unsure as to what to do next. We're just holding hands and smiling and you know what, it's a really nice feeling.

Liz breaks the spell by downing the last of her Chablis and asks, "Shall we open another?"
To which I sensibly reply, "Can we get something to eat first?"

And so, my epic Bank Holiday continues with a pizza delivery and a couple more glasses of a heavenly dry white wine. We both flirt with a discussion on the practicalities of speaking to her lawyer and how to break the news to Matt but, as the alcohol takes the edge off of things, the flirting is increasingly with one another.

Eventually and perhaps inevitably, Liz's rough week catches up with her. At the point where she is leaning back against me and relaxing into my welcoming shoulder her eyes begin to glaze over and her breathing slows down. When her heads flops to one side and I am sure that she has sunk into unconsciousness, I let go of my own inner tension and lay back with a huge smile on my face.

The next thing I know, the room is in semi-darkness. I check my watch and make a quick calculation that something over two hours has past. I also become aware of the sound of a toilet flushing and realise that it was Liz's departure that must have disturbed my slumbering. She switches on the side lights and makes for the balcony for a cigarette as I rouse myself from the sofa. I decide that it is time to let her be for a while and head home. She thanks me for coming over and gives me another hug but still our lips do not come together.

Walking back across the park, I pass the bench that I had sat on earlier in the day and feel the need to repeat the experience. The park has changed with the passing of the sun and I am acutely aware that something has changed in me too. There is a calmness that I feel in just seeing this through and waiting for Liz to extrapolate herself from the mess that she's in. Then, yes *then*, I hope ... no, I *believe*, it will all come good.

It's the shorter working week which always makes for a good reason to be cheerful when you turn up on a Tuesday but, on this particular morning, I get a couple of comments from my equally jovial colleagues concerning my new found positivity. As I am reluctant to satisfy their curiosity by recounting events since we shut up shop on Friday, I feign disbelief at their insinuations and so leave them guessing. However, I do feel the need to share my thoughts with someone that I can entrust them to, so my session with Abi this afternoon is very well timed.

Don't get me wrong, I am still concerned for Liz and definitely wouldn't want to be in her shoes. All I'm saying is that, well, to be perfectly honest - as I know I can be with you - I feel like someone has turned the light back on or, as the song goes, "I can see clearly now, the rain has gone".

At the appointed hour, I join Abi for another thoroughly enjoyable session with her exciting and excitable group. The experience proves to be therapeutic for me as I find that it has temporarily cleared my mind of all the stuff that I wanted to speak to my friend about. When, finally, we are alone in the large empty space of the hall, I get yet another enquiry about the change in my demeanour.

"Am I not normally such a happy chappie?" I throw back at her, hoping for an honest opinion.
"Well ..." The pause in her response is an answer in itself.
"Ok, ok. I guess you're right. I've been really worried about Liz lately. But, I think all that's going to change now. So, yes, things are looking up."
Abi doesn't seem to be quite sure about my explanation and probes me further, "Change how?"

"I'm not sure I know that myself yet; she's been up front about what's happening and I think she has got her head around the best way to handle her problems though. What's really good about it is that she wants me to be there for her, instead of that waste of space, Matt."

I finish my sentence with a hint of triumphalism in my voice; it does not escape Abi's notice.

"You're going to have to spell it all out for me Andy; it sounds as if a lot has happened over the weekend. Listen, I'm supposed to be meeting Tom in the George & Dragon in about ten minutes. Why don't you head off and have a blokey chat with him while I finish off here? I'll be along later." Abi holds the door open for me and ushers me out.

"Right you are. Don't be too long though ... otherwise we'll end talking about boats all evening."

"He'll like that." She smiles and then disappears from view behind the closing door.

Sweet; I'm heading to a great pub after work. What could be better? On arrival, I avail myself of the guest ale and find Tom out back with a pint of the same.

"What's it like?" I want to know his opinion before I start into mine.

"It's very nice ... not too strong but still quite tasty."

After taking the top off and swallowing the first mouthful, I concur, "Mmmm, not bad."

"Good to see you Andy, I assume Abi told you I'd be here."

"Yeah, yeah, I just left her, she'll be over shortly."

"Great. Are you in a rush or can you stay and have a meal with us?" Tom kindly suggests.

"No, I've got no plans. I'll stay, thanks. And thanks again for Saturday too."

"Well, let's hope there are plenty more days like that in the future." Tom cheerfully toasts by raising his glass.

"Amen to that." I reciprocate.

Before too long, our conversation has turned from sailing to more personal matters.

"How did you feel about our get together on Sunday, Andy?"

"Well, it was different; it looks like a lot of fun."

"Anything that particularly interested you?" Tom asks, knowingly.

I wouldn't have been surprised if he had nudged me or winked. But no, he patiently waits for my response as I lean back in my chair. Do I take the bait? Yes, I do.

"If you mean Mel, then yes, she did make an impression on me."

"A good one, I hope." Tom confides.

"Yeah, for sure; I'll be seeing her again at the weekend, in fact. It's a bit hard to judge after such a brief introduction but I'm sure we'll get on ok. Truth is though Tom, I don't know if I'm ready for someone new yet; my life feels complicated enough right now."

"Well, like you say, you've only just been introduced so I'm sure Mel won't be rushing you down the aisle just yet!" Tom smiles as he humours me.

"No, you're right ... taking myself too seriously again."

We both reflect briefly as we enjoy the flavour of the hops.

"Where's the complication in your life, if you don't mind me asking?" Tom resumes.

"Oh, I'm just a bit confused about a relationship that may or may not be over. The thing is, I'm not very good at being just friends when I still really want to be with her. You and Abi seem to be so sure about one another; I wish it was like that with me and Liz." I confess.

"Oh, I wouldn't want you to think that we have all the answers; it's still early days for us ... but it sounds as if you already have history with Liz. Maybe a friendship would be a much better outcome, in the long run?"

"Hmmm ... you might be right, you might be right." I linger over my reply and contemplate the possibility.

"Right about what?" Abi chimes in, having just arrived and caught me musing.

"Tom was reminding me that a friendship is something worth having."

Tom gets up and greets Abi before he heads off to get another round in. Abi takes a seat and places a re-assuring hand on my arm. When we are all sitting comfortably, I recount the essential facts relating to Liz's tale of woe; my willingness to get involved and my unconcealed enthusiasm in telling it do not go down well.

Abi looks at Tom. Tom looks at Abi and then they both look at me.
Tom speaks. "Andy, if I ask you a straight quest, will you give me a straight answer?"
I'm a little worried but I agree.
"Do you want to go away with Liz when this is all over?"
It's a good question but not an easy one to answer.
"Oooh, now, that's not a straight answer kinda question." I protest.
Indeed, in the course of our meal I deftly manage to avoid giving one. I can sense their concern but I remain unsure as to whether they are disappointed in me or sad at the prospect of our brief friendship coming to an end. Time will tell.

Chapter 6

With a modicum of nervous anticipation, I dutifully ring Mel on the Saturday. It is a reassuring feeling as it confirms that it means something to me; I am genuinely excited at the prospect of meeting up and spending some time together. Nevertheless, I try hard not to come across as overenthusiastic, in case it scares her off! Anyway, I have no such problems and within a few minutes our conversation is developing quite naturally into something very enjoyable.

Eventually, I suggest that we try out a restaurant in North Street that one of my work colleagues had kindly recommended to me recently. Mel says that she too had heard good things about it, so I rang to book a table as soon as we've finished our chat.

So, everything seems to be coming together quite nicely and I take myself off to the Leisure Centre to chill out in the pool for a while. My thoughts run a little wild as I plough my way up and down, up and down. However, in the evening, as I smarten myself up and prepare to make my way into town, I remind myself that I should resist my natural impulses and just enjoy the moment. Finally, I check myself in the mirror, put a smile on my face and set off on a new adventure.

My arrival is perfectly punctual, as is Mel's, and we enter *Amelie and Friends* following a courteous continental greeting. Mel has managed to look stunning, while not appearing overdressed, and her perfume smells divine. She thanks me for the complement that I pay her as we wait to be seated.

I could say that Mel is enthralled by my combination of witticisms and enthralling stories but the truth is that it was the other way around. With every mouthful of delicious food that I consume, I find my appreciation of her many faceted personality increasing as I listen to her in sheer delight.

We begin on safe ground, singing Abi's praises and comparing our experiences of the invaluable assistance we have both received on arrival in Chichester; mine through work and hers through the church that she had visited within the first few weeks. I hadn't realised that Mel was also new in town – but how could I? Abi's ingenuity in putting us together seems to make more sense.

I don't think there is any conscious decision to do so but, quite seamlessly, the story of her journey here unravels itself. The children's entertainment project with the puppet show was something that she jumped at the chance of getting involved with. Mel explains that the use of play is an invaluable tool in her line of work and to be able to do something so joyful in her spare time just helps her no end. From there she goes on to tell me about the project she was affiliated to that had brought her to the city. She works with children and their parents but outside of the NHS now. She stayed in Southampton after graduating and gained five years of wonderful experience there before she had decided that it was time to move on and spread her wings a bit more. A similar impulse had brought her down from Lincolnshire when she was choosing which University to apply to.

Her life has been a happy one and she is looking to build on her experience until the time is right to start her own practice. Whether that will be here or elsewhere just depends on how settled she feels but, so far, she is liking her new surroundings. That's the abridged version, anyway. There are no revelations as to any deeply meaningful relationships, just a real sense of purpose and compassion for the people whose lives she touches.

I throw in a few of my own thoughts where I deemed it to be appropriate but I am left with a slight tinge of regret that I had not been as focused. I wonder whether, at some point, she had been close to deciding on a more hedonistic lifestyle. I'm sure that she would have attracted a great deal of attention with her svelte figure and naturally blonde hair. I keep these thoughts to myself. I also begin to think that, maybe, I am much more indebted to Abi than I had realised; my presence in this restaurant, with this woman and at this moment, is a minor miracle.

While Mel is enjoying her dessert, she listens to me as I gave her the lowdown on a production that is coming to the theatre at the end of the month. To my pleasant surprise she enthusiastically indicates her interest in coming to see the show and says how much she loves live performances. I'm beginning to suspect that this relationship might be going somewhere by time we are sipping coffee and my hopes are raised even further when Mel takes out her diary to arrange another date.

Despite my protestations, Mel insists on paying half of the bill. No gender stereotyping where she is concerned. A feeling of relaxation and bonhomie encompasses us as we say goodnight to the waitress and make our way out into the street. Quite naturally, I find myself placing my hand into the small of Mel's back as I go. It slips away as she turns to face me once we have joined the other Saturday night revellers. She thanks me for a lovely evening and kisses me on the cheek. There is no doubt in my mind that this is the end of our time together; she heads off in the direction of the Market Cross. For a few seconds I watch her go, enjoying the wiggle in her walk. She turns, smiles and, with an amiable little wave, calls out, "See you on Friday." I raise my hand in acknowledgement and return to admiring her movements until she is swallowed up by the night people.

Well, my head is spinning as I amble back home. I take my time and enjoy replaying some of the evening's highlights in my mind. I sleep soundly and am sorely tempted to hop on a train to Southampton and spend a day checking out the city. But, wisely, I come to my senses and decide that that would be taking things a little too far.

But the idea of exploring has gripped me, so I take myself off to Brighton instead. I have to confess that I did consider asking Liz to join me but what I really need is a bit of space and anyway, I haven't heard from her all week.

I succumb to temptation by midweek and have a strong sense of déjà-vu after I leaving another message, visiting the shop and calling at Liz's flat; I am none the wiser for it. Except that is, for having another very nice chat with Beth who is pleased to tell me her plans for the shop, now that she is going to be taking it over.

This time, however, I am ok about it; I can just let it ride. Eventually, later that day, Liz returns my call and tells me that she is being "looked after" by her folks up at the "the house". Her dad has been assisting her in planning for the future and she is glad to be safely out of the way for a while. I am happy to hear it. She also tells me she'll be back in town after the weekend to face her day in court and invites me over to keep her company on the night before. I gladly accept.

And so, to Friday evening's fun and games. I have to say, I do love the sound of the pins being regularly decimated at a busy bowling alley. As soon as you walk through the doors, the music's playing, the lights on the game machines are flashing away and I just feel SO in need of a beer from the poorly lit bar. Happily, I find that Mel, Abi and Tom have all gravitated into the refreshment area too so I'm treated to a pint of Guinness by Tom.

It's a great start to a lovely evening, I have to say. None of us are particularly good at bowling but that's not the point really, is it? It's not much fun if you take it too seriously, unless you take it very seriously and then have the enjoyment of getting very high scores. Anyway, what I'm trying to say is, I didn't win. I should say that WE didn't win as Tom & Abi thrashed Mel and me, then the girls narrowly defeated the boys to make Abi the overall champion. Abi offers to get another round in at the Richmond Arms down by the canal and nobody has any objection.

An hour or so of friendly chat in a lively Friday night crowd would normally end in my excessive alcohol consumption making it difficult for me to navigate my way home. But this night, I want to be lucid and ready for anything. So, we're all relaxed and coherent when Tom and Abi take their leave of us on the ring road; hugs all round. This gives me the opportunity to enquire where Mel lives and make my offer to accompany her which, I'm glad to hear, she accepts. It's a bit out of my way but the night is still young. As we walk, we swap our ideas about which area of the city we'd rather live in and we're soon standing on the threshold of Mel's flat in a strangely Antipodean named street. I can see why she said that she's quite content with her choice of accommodation.

As it looks likely that I'm about to make my way back to my equally satisfactory abode, my attention turns to the pressing question of how amorous a departure it's going to be. However, as she looks for her keys, Mel invites me in and I am soon being treated to Mel's favourite liquor coffee; a cosy chat ensues. Despite the alcohol, my best effort at paying her complements and general conversation steering there is no point at which a physical coming together results. Mel was quite relaxed and confident in her own space and I come away feeling pleased that I'd been allowed into her home. But, as I sloped off under the glare of the streetlights, I have to ask myself a familiar question, "What was that about?"

In the morning, on reflection, I feel that progress had been made and I just need to be patient. Maybe I could learn something here: there is no need to be in such a hurry. We are all meeting up again next weekend. "It's all good." I tell myself.

Two weeks ago I remember thinking, "Time will tell." Those two weeks have revealed very little, sadly. I'm taking my favourite walk again, over to Liz's place. Tomorrow is her day in court and I'm her hero. Glad to be of service but, if anything, the waters are muddier than ever.

Liz is expecting me and up I go. I must be disciplined and put Liz's needs before my own, for the next twenty four hours at least. Liz greets me with the customary friendly hug and my first impressions are good. There is no alcohol on the table and she's looking pretty together. We have coffee and Liz takes me through to her spacious and inviting bedroom to obtain my approval on her choice of clothing for her big day in court. Neither of us has been in a situation where we're facing a judgment; not in this way, anyhow. So, there's a nervous excitement that clouds Liz's inner turmoil.

After an hour or more of discussing various potential outcomes, we settle into a very pleasant time watching *Inception* on Blu-ray; a film we have watched together before and will, no doubt, both enjoy this time around. Half way through the film, Liz takes a cushion and plants it in my lap before very deliberately stretching out on the sofa and resting her head on it. A brief thought of Mel is quickly put aside as I begin to run my fingers through Liz's hair. A memory of what happened the last time I was in this exact same scenario is not so hastily dispensed with. Liz indicates her approval by softly stating, "That's nice".

Thanks to my new found iron will or possibly an interest in the *long game outcome* I restrict my contact to the cranium and see out the end of the movie. There is silence in the room and Liz is slipping into a peaceful sleep and I savour the moment. It's getting on for eleven o'clock however and I suggest to Liz that she make her way to bed and get a decent night's kip. I depart with a goodnight kiss and return home to do likewise.

Even though Liz's hearing is in the morning, I decide that it would be prudent to take the whole day off from work. The fallout from the experience, for me as much as for Liz, could be difficult to deal with. Abi is the only person from the theatre that knows anything about my whereabouts on the day and I'm pleased to get an encouraging text from her as I head down South Street towards the Court.

Architectural speaking, the building is not one of Chichester's greatest attractions. It's red, it's brick and it's functional but hey, it's no amusement arcade. What's more, the proceedings are equally functional. No high octane court drama story to relate to you here, I'm afraid. Liz and I make eye contact once things get underway and everyone is respectful and courteous, as they should be. As Liz is changing her plea to guilty, there is nothing to argue over and the magistrate is inclined to be lenient in view of her admission and her previously unblemished record. Her father's lawyer was spot on in predicting that she'd walk away with a fine and not even a particularly large one. However, Liz knows that she now has a criminal record and that will be far more of a problem.

Unsurprisingly, none of Liz's drug taking friends are with me to support her. Neither is her old man, who is away on business. Beth would have attended but couldn't find anybody to mind the shop. So, after an outpouring of genuine thanks from the two of us to her lawyer, we're left alone on the busy street. The world is rushing around us, as if nothing important had occurred but for us, the nightmare is over. We stop by at the shop for Liz to let Beth know that she hasn't been incarcerated and then just lay on the grass in front of the Cathedral. Time to enjoy the freedom.

There is nothing quite like laying flat on the grass with a friend and looking up at the sky. The world disappears, momentarily, and the vastness of all that air and emptiness somehow removes all concerns from your mind. Well, my mind; I can't be sure what's going on in Liz's mind. She's been having some good thoughts about me obviously. Next thing I know, I feel her roll gently up against my side and places her hand on my check in order to turn my face towards her. I'm treated to a lingering kiss and a few blissful minutes of her affections. I put up no resistance but I felt afterwards that such a public display should have been avoided, maybe, in case anyone we know happened to be passing by.

Sated, Liz returns her gaze skyward and takes in the towering spire and the rainclouds that are gathering around it. She jumps up and suggests that we shelter inside as the first spits and spots descend and lightly brush her skin. I'm going wherever she leads me, so in we go. With neither of us having entered this sacred space before this day, we set about exploring the dark corners and light spaces with increasing fascination and an hour slips by. Making our way out to the Cloisters Cafe for a light lunch, I finally feel able to speak freely to Liz; I ask her where she wants to go from here but it is apparent that she has no particular plans.

The steady rain that has set in averts any inclination toward a relaxing outdoor pursuit and Liz is beginning to show some signs of weariness following her ordeal. I suggest that I accompany her back to her flat where she can rest and then freshen up before I pick her up for a few celebratory beverages in the evening. I'm being masterful and caring and it's all working out a treat. Until, that is, I return to her flat, as arranged, at seven o'clock.

My assumption that a beautifully adorned creature with a beaming smile on her face would greet me was way off the mark as I stood on the threshold, utterly confounded. A dishevelled being in a loose top and trackie bottoms, eighties rock chic hair and smeared mascara let me in and waddled away. I followed. I wondered what Liz might have been taking but there was no obvious evidence that she wasn't stone cold sober. It struck me that, on this occasion, the cold light of reality may be the cause of Liz's difficulties.

Liz plonked herself down on the sofa and took a tissue to wipe her nose; I think she'd been crying.

"Sorry Andy, I thought about ringing to save you the journey ... but I just couldn't face spending the evening on my own."

"Hey, it's what friends are for; I couldn't leave you on your own like this." I reassured her. "Why don't you go and sort yourself out while I fix us a drink? Tea or coffee?"

Hey presto, five minutes later, Liz no longer looks like an extra from a low budget horror movie and we're out on the balcony, tea in hand. The rainclouds have moved on and there is a freshness in the evening air that carries a hint of the wet streets below. People are getting to where they're going for the night but we won't be joining them.

"Matt rang." Liz blurts out to initiate a cathartic rationalization of her situation. "It wasn't pleasant. He wanted to come over but I told him not to. I also told him that I hadn't mentioned his name in court, so if anything did come back on him, in wouldn't be down to me. He seemed happy with that. But I'm going to have to tell him some time."

"Tell him what, exactly?"

"That we're finished." Liz elucidates without hesitation and with no apparent emotion. But the illusion is only temporary; she hangs her head and then the tears start to flow once more. "It's finished ... all of it." She sobs.

I move the mugs out of harm's way and run a comforting hand up and down her spine, giving her the opportunity to just let go of her anxiety. There is nothing else to do or say right now but I'm thinking about it.

At some point, the tension I can feel in Liz's back muscles melts away and I begin to think that, maybe, it's time to talk. However, she grabs hold of the balcony rail and pushes her torso away from it, creating an inverted arch in her back that stretches out her inner tension to the max. Holding the pose, she takes a deep breath and blows it out, slowly, before standing up straight to face me.

"Do you know what I need?" She says.
I'd seen a bottle of Champagne in the fridge earlier and assumed she was thinking of that. "A glass or two of shampoo?" I venture.
Now, given the circumstances, I am not prepared for what happens next. In fact, if a mate was relating this to me, confidentially, I would probably raise an eyebrow. But I am going with her all the way on this one.

She takes my hand and leads me back inside. The champagne is still an option, I think. She takes me into the kitchen. Yes, champagne, it must be. She pops herself up on the work surface, opens her legs and gathers me in. Her legs wrap around me and her hands caress my neck and shoulders as our mouths come together with a lustful hunger.

As our tongues reacquaint themselves in their passionate dance, I feel under Liz's loose top. I had already ascertained that she has nothing on underneath it and my hands explore any and all of her warm smooth body that can be reached until she quickly slips it off over her head and we resume where we had left off. My roaming hands slip under her bottom and she leans into me, transferring her weight through her arms on to the back of my neck. Gripping me hard with her thighs, I am able to slide her out of her elevated location and then manoeuvre my grip so that I can hold her gorgeous buttocks in hand as I carry her into the bedroom.

Finished? No, we are just getting started.

Chapter 7

If there's a better way to wake up than feeling the warm arm of a beautiful, naked woman pulling you closer, then I'd like to know what it is: I'll definitely give it a try. Sadly, despite the huge temptation to ring in and *pull a sickie*, my better nature won out and I found myself dressing for the short walk home around 8 AM.

Anything and everything seemed possible. I kissed Liz lingeringly on the lips and she playfully hung on to me as I bid her farewell. With one last contented look at her gorgeous form sprawling across the King size bed, we exchanged a smile of satisfaction and I made my way out of the building. The fresh memories of Liz's scent and the refreshing morning breeze elevated my sense of well-being and I floated all the way back to my front door.

I didn't have time for breakfast but I was unconcerned; food was of minor importance. Even arriving at the office twenty minutes late did not prompt any pang of conscience. My furtive texting with Liz kept me going for a couple of hours until I took myself outside for a solitary, cadged cigarette. The grumbling of my stomach slowly began to attract my attention as the morning hours slipped by and I took myself off for an early lunch. Liz had not suggested a rendezvous and I had decided to play along with whatever course she chose, for the time being. It was while I sat in the Bishops Palace Gardens, munching through my cheese & pickle sandwich that a serious dilemma germinated in one of my serotonin drenched brain cells. Which adult male could I enjoy sharing my cosmic experience with?

I'm pretty sure that Matt would be a VERY bad choice. I tried to conjure up a scenario in which that would work … because, actually, I do really WANT to tell Matt. I even pictured a scene reminiscent of the farewell scene in Casablanca. But, this didn't work unless I told a big fat lie and gave up on my future with Liz. It would have to be someone else then. Tom was my next best option; there were even more reasons why that too was a bad idea. It hit me then.

All the good stuff that had been happening in my private life in the past few weeks and the potential for some sound, reliable relationships was all about to go out of the window. I asked myself, how am I going to explain my change of direction to Abi? I told myself that I hadn't made Mel any promises and that, being a modern woman, she would take it in her stride. Maybe Tom would be happy for me, even if it did change his opinion of me for the worse.

By the time I had calmed down and rationalised the situation, it was time to head back to the Theatre. For now, I hope, it will be my little secret. I just need to let things lie for a few days, see out the week and check in with Liz to see how she wants to play things. For all I know it may have been a one off and nobody will be any the wiser, if I just say nothing. In any case, if I can't share it, I am sure going to enjoy relishing the moment!

Thursday evening passed peacefully, except for my slightly obsessional activity of checking my mobile every twenty minutes. It's true, we hadn't made any arrangements to repeat our night of passion but I had hoped that Liz would begin to feel an irresistible need for my presence as the darkness descended. I certainly felt the desire to ring her but, knowing the fragile state she was in, I didn't want to blow my chances by pushing too hard too soon. A simple text, wishing her *sweet dreams* as I turned in, received a swift and positive response that helped me to catch up on lost sleep.

Thankfully, I catch up with Abi whilst performing our duties on Friday. So much has changed since our paths had crossed earlier in the week but I stick resolutely to my decision. Ok, yes, I lie to Abi. I make out that I was the Good Samaritan by helping Liz out after the Court case but say nothing about what followed. It is easily done and anyway, she has a far greater secret to tell than mine.

"Well done you." She says. "She's lucky to have you as a friend, Andy."

I can only smile, coyly, before she begins to tease me about her big news.

"Are you busy tomorrow night?"

"Oh, I was leaving a space in my diary, just for you Abi." I joke.

"Good, coz we're hitting Thursdays for a little celebration .... and you are invited."

"I am? What are we celebrating, exactly?"

Abi is acting strangely, akin to Bilbo Baggins. I am half expecting her to present me with a riddle. Then the penny drops; she withdraws her hand from her pocket to display her hand, replete with a small diamond on a silver band.

"Very nice". I say. "Who's the lucky fella?"

She knows I am only playing with her but still answers the question.

"Tom, of course ... and I'm the lucky girl, I think."

After allowing me a suitably respectful period for examination of said valuable item, we agree that we definitely need time to chat. I accept her invitation to the club tomorrow night and Abi suggests that I ask Liz if she would like to join us. She thinks she might like to let her hair down after a difficult week. I agree that it's a good idea. I spend the rest of the day wondering whether it is or not. Then, I sleep on it.

In the morning, I procrastinate and wonder why Liz hasn't bothered to contact me yet. There is only one way to find out; I ring her. My call goes straight to voicemail so I conclude that her phone is turned off or she is somewhere inaccessible. I don't leave a message but send a text, "Hi, call me if you want to have some fun with me tonight XXX."

I decide that I need to preload for my night out and down a couple of cans of G&T that were cooling in the fridge before setting off. As Liz hasn't got back to me, it feels like a good evening for a leisurely stroll to the Eastgate to catch a bus out of town. Arriving around dusk will be fine, I think. My decision to wander past Liz's block on the chance that I might run into her, accidently like, proves to be a major mistake however.

I watch the sky darken as we rattle along toward my destination. I send Abi a text as the urban sprawl turns, almost miraculously, into green pastures to say that I will be there in ten. In the twilight, I pick my way around the lake that stands between me and the sparkling lights until I join the dribble of revellers who are similarly energised by the sound of music.

Once inside, I survey the predominantly female participants on the dancefloor in the hope of picking out Abi from the crowd. I enjoy the sensation of watching the shapes gyrating in time with the rhythm but cannot see anyone recognisable so I head for the bar. Before I have achieved my objective of getting served, I feel a hand on my back and a familiar face greets me as I turn to see if my luck is in: it is Tom's. He is just getting a round in himself and kindly asks me what I am drinking, so as to add to his order. In return, I help him carry the numerous alcoholic units of various hues up on to the balcony where their crowd has gathered. It fells good to be welcomed into the spontaneous joy of these confident young adults.

After getting a lingering hug from Abi, I look around and pick out a couple of familiar faces; none of which are Mel's. Somewhere, deep down, I am aware of the relief that this brings. But, to maintain the illusion of normality, I express by disappointment when Abi tells me that Mel hasn't been able to change her plans and join us at such short notice. Pushing on past my show of interest, I am immediately invited to make up a foursome during the week. We leave it at that and subsequently find myself being dragged off to demonstrate my inability to look cool on the dancefloor. I don't care though; I'm in the right mood to just let go of all the recent events in my life. This night is about celebrating the happiness of my two friends.

As I twist and turn in a way that I consider reasonably in time with the music, a wry smile forms on my face as I acknowledge the ludicrous position I have managed to get myself into. How it will turn out, I have no idea. Just to get a few beers down me and dance the night away with a good crowd is sufficient.

My stamina completely goes after a particularly energetic five minutes enjoying a song that I actually recognise, even if the artist is a total mystery to me. Conceding defeat, I make for the bar to see if I can afford to treat Tom, Abi and their friends to a bottle of something fizzy. I am in luck. I even have a suitably attired gentleman assigned to bring it up to us.

Sliding my card securely back into my wallet, I realised that I am being stared at by the imposing figure beside me. My heart sinks when he speaks and the figure and voice homogenise, unmistakeably, into Matt.

"What are we celebrating?" He asks.
"An engagement." I tell him, cheerfully.
"Oh … not yours, surely?" He replies, cynically.
"I should be so lucky." I shout, as the music suddenly ramps up a notch. My fear of being left with no option but to invite him to join our party are steadily increasing too. Uncertain of Matt's intentions, I turn the questions on to him."
"What brings you here then?"
The answer is surprising, "I followed you, as it happens."
I let out a nervous snigger. "Really? Why?"
"I had something I wanted to give you. Coming outside for a fag?"

Very worried now; but I can't think of a plausible reason not to.

Once outside I follow Matt, sheep like, into the gloom over by the lake. There, Matt makes his intentions very clear by placing a sharp blow to my groin via a firm upward movement of his right knee. As I pitch forward in agony, he follows it up with a firm fist to the left side of my face and I crumple in a heap. Gobsmacked, quite literally. I vaguely recall a stream of expletives directed at me as I silently hope that I'm not going to receive a good kicking too. Another thought is, "Where's a doorman when you really need one?"

I get the gist of Matt's verbal assault; he wishes me to desist from sleeping with his girlfriend and to avoid all contact with either of them, forthwith. I am thankful for small mercies when he disappears into the darkness without inflicting any further pain.

It takes a minute to regain my composure and I remain in the foetal position until the desire to sit up outweighs the necessity to hold my genitals, in the vain hope of it reducing the agony. An inspection of my face with my hand revealed a fat top lip and a slightly bloody tear but all of my teeth are still in place. It isn't long before I can stagger off in the same direction as Matt. With a glance back into the light, I can see that the doormen were occupied with checking through another wave of cheerful punters. Matt had been clever; I hadn't.

I know that I will be missed back inside by now. It cheers me up, slightly, to think of them opening up the surprise that I had laid on and trying to find me to share in it. But hey, I'm not about to spoil their evening by making a scene. As I make my weary way home, I contemplate the scenarios in which Liz may have imparted the truth about recent events to her splendid beau. Most of all, I hope that his idea of retribution has been altogether less physical with her. However, on the upside, if it means that the final curtain has fallen on their romance then I'd have a free run. But then, remembering

Matt's vitriolic outburst, it doesn't seem like he was viewing it that way. One thing is crystal clear; I need to speak to Liz, *tout suite.*

1

Throughout my short and shambolic adult life I have, up until now anyway, been quite proud of the fact that I have not woken up with a bruised cheek and sore mouth to reflect upon in the bathroom mirror. The state of my face isn't as bad as the pain suggests so a day on the white tablets and a little seclusion with a possible sickie tomorrow will resolve matters quite nicely, I think. Nobody will be any the wiser if I just make a couple of calls and nurse my wounds.
I'd had the presence of mind to send Abi a text during my solitary, crestfallen journey back to the safety of my residence last night. I doubted that my lame excuse for buggering off without saying goodbye would satisfy anyone with half an ounce of intelligence though. I also had a strong desire to be totally honest, having disliked the sensation of hiding the truth from her. But that could wait for now.

First things first; track down Liz and try to get some clarification on the current situation. Evidently, I am unlikely to like what I hear and maybe this would be a really good time to back off. But no … *in for a penny, in for a pound.* Here goes.

It's ringing … it's answered.
"Hi." Says a soft, uncertain voice.
"Hi." I reply with empathetic uncertainty. "How's it going?"
"Hmmm. Not so good."
"How about, I come over this afternoon and you can tell me all about it?"
"No … not today Andy, I had a late one last night. I'll call you tomorrow night; I promise."
What can I say? I can wait another twenty four hours, surely. "OK. Take care."

"Bye."

Oh well; that's progress, of a sort. We are communicating again and I have a day in which to think over what it is that I want to say. Which is what, exactly?

I mull things over while consuming my lunch and then put in the regular Sunday afternoon call to the folks back home. Following this conversation, I discover a surprising resolution to my earlier ponderings. What picture had I painted to my mother of her happy and contented son? Not one that had included anything that I had experienced in the last seven days. In fact, our little chat had been much less genial than the previous one. Since then, I had managed to burrow my way into a dark hole; like a blind little mole, I was just going to keep on digging.

With the thought of coming up for air fresh on my mind, the doorbell rings: an unexpected guest. For a second, I recoil at the prospect of Matt on my doorstep. Trusting it to be a friendly face, I answer the call.

"Hellooow." I say, in lingering surprise at Tom's presence.

"Hello." He says, leaning slightly to the right and frowning as he takes a better look at my bruised features. "Is this a good time? Thought I'd stop by to see if you were ok."

"Yeah, sure; it's really not as bad as it looks. Come on in."

I lead Tom into the kitchen.

"This is very nice." He says as he views the back garden through the window.

"No, not bad, is it? Tea?"

"Yes, thanks Andy."

Tom starts to recount his tales of the great night that I missed as I brew up and is still regaling me with the highlights as we make ourselves comfortable in the lounge. It's good of him to resist asking me any direct questions about the rest of my evening and eventually he remembers the Champagne surprise; I confirm that is was from me.

"What a shame you couldn't stay to enjoy it." He says.
"Well, believe me that would have been my preferred option ... if only ..."

Where to begin? Not at the beginning; that would be tedious. How about the last time we spoke?

"You see Tom, I bumped into a friend while I was at the bar. Well, not really a friend ... not now, anyway. So, we went outside for a little chat and I was coming straight back in; but, as it turns out, he wasn't in the mood for talking ... and ... what he did was ... he, er, assaulted me."
"What on earth for?"
"It's a bit complicated but, in a nutshell, he thought there was something going on between me and his girlfriend."
"Oh, so he was way off the mark." Tom assumed.
A pregnant pause ensued.
"Tom, I'm not going to lie to you; actually, no, he wasn't."
Whatever Tom's thinking, he's keeping it to himself. I, on the other hand, feel the need to justify myself.
"The thing is: I totally believe that Liz would be far better off without him and I was just trying to help her out. I didn't realise it would go this far. I reckon it's me that's in a mess now."
"Well that's one way of looking at it." I am advised.
I let this thought percolate into the infusion that is brewing in my consciousness. Tom seems reassuringly comfortable with observing my contemplations. We share a quite profound silence as we consume our beverages in unison.
"Another way of looking at it", he continues, "would be to say that you'd be better off without Liz and ask yourself who might be there to help you out."
Although this is not an earth shatteringly new idea or one without some appeal on one level, a part of me rails against it; I find myself going to the window just to break the tension.
"Isn't it a bit late for that?" I ask, looking up at the sky.

"I wouldn't say so; in fact, I'd say that this is precisely the right time."

Turning back to my guest, I throw up another line of defence, "Easier said than done."

"No, if I were in your shoes Andy, I'd think carrying on the way you are would be the hardest thing to do."

"Yeah, but you've got Abi; you're great together, anyone can see that." I continue to resist.

"No, you're right; I'm not in your shoes right now but I have been there, believe me."

"It just doesn't sit well with me, giving in to that thug. Why should I let him dictate to me?" I wonder.

"You don't have to; YOU make YOUR OWN choice." Tom encourages me. "You can turn your back on it just because you decide it's what you want to do. End of."

I sit back down again and begin to seriously consider the potential of the argument.

Tom continues, "And if you're serious about it, then I'm sure that certain people will pick up on it."

"You think?"

"Yeah, showing some genuine repentance could go a long way." Tom advocates.

"We are talking about Mel here, aren't we? I'd given that up as a totally lost cause."

"Well, you certainly haven't done yourself any favours! But, as far as I understand, you two weren't actually together, were you? Like I say, a bit of bridge building …"

"More like excavating the Channel Tunnel, I'd say." Which I did.

"It's just a question of which road you want to walk down Andy."

Thankfully, we drop the subject, so I can relax and enjoy Tom telling me about the plans that he and Abi are making for the future. I'm really happy for him. Eventually, he realises that time is getting on; he makes to leave and get back to Abi. As he goes, he once again encourages me to think positively about what he'd said earlier.

"We'll be praying for you." Tom confides.

Grinning, I respond, "Well, I need all the help I can get."

Tom just smiles and lays a friendly hand on my shoulder.

I close the door behind him and just hope I'll be left in peace until tomorrow.

Chapter 8

Monday, Monday; there are so many songs about Monday! Despite Tom's encouraging words yesterday, I still can't quite steel myself to fess up to my colleagues about the alteration to my facial features. So, I phone in with a sob story in the hope that it won't look half so bad by the time Tuesday dawns.

My proximity to the office precludes any daytime excursions on the off-chance of being observed and my little subterfuge unravelling. Despite my misgivings at wasting the opportunity, I convince myself that this is no bad thing; I need to give some serious thought to Tom's words of wisdom yesterday and at least try to decide what I want to say to Liz later on. It proves to be a much bigger challenge than I had anticipated but making some space for some quiet reflection actually turns out to be a positive experience. Somehow, a still small voice inside finally got to be heard. Will it be the one that triumphs over adversity? We shall see.

As the rush of traffic eases at the end of the working day, I escape from my four walled seclusion to stretch my legs and prepare myself for a conversation that I could not possibly have envisaged seven days ago. On returning, I refresh myself with a splash of cold water from the bathroom basin. The two sides of my face appear to be much more alike as I examine my reflection in the mirror.

With mounting anxiety, I flick through my CD collection in search of something soothing. My quest is thwarted by the sudden interruption of my ringtone. The caller is identified as Liz; I swipe the small screen. Here goes.

"Andy, I can't tell you how sorry I am. I bet you're pretty p'd off with all this, aren't you?" Liz jumps in, skipping any niceties. There's a hint of anxiety in her tone.

"Well, I've had better weeks. How's yours been?"

"Oh, I can't begin to describe it … just bizarre." She replies.

"No, go on; fill me in Liz, I'm all ears." I insist, resolved to discover the truth.

"Ok, so ... after you left on Thursday, I went in to the shop. I was a bit late but it didn't matter much because I was on a bit of a high. It was good day with Beth and we had a good laugh; you know, when I'm there I can just forget about everything and focus on what I love. Anyhow, who do you think should be waiting for me when I got back?"

"Matt?" I hazard a guess.

"Too right. Somehow, he already knew about my fine. I wouldn't be surprised if he had someone checking up on me; making sure I didn't say anything incriminating. Obviously, I hadn't, so he was all sweetness and light. He wanted to come up so we could talk and *sort things out* but I wasn't going to let him off that easy. It took me about twenty minutes before I managed to get him to leave."

A pause for thought and then she continues, "I was thinking of you Andy. You wouldn't think much of me, if I was to treat what happened last week as insignificant, would you? Coz it wasn't."

"No, it wasn't; not for me. Did you tell him about us?"

"I had no intention to; what business of his was it anyway? As far as I was concerned, we'd split ... permanently. He didn't see it that way though. He was waiting for me again on Friday and I just lost it with him."

"And?" I prompt.

"And ... I wanted to give him a good reason to leave me alone."

"So you told him." I conclude.

Liz didn't need to reply; at that moment I could easily envisage events unfolding, leading to the assault and battery on my face and testicles. I wasn't about to lay the blame on her but there were nagging doubts in my mind.

"It doesn't appear to have worked Liz."

"What doesn't?" She asks, indicating to me that her mind is elsewhere.

"Matt ... he hasn't left you alone, has he?"

"No."
Expecting something a little more eloquent, I resist the urge to dive in with another question. But the silence is beginning to feel a little uncomfortable by the time the next two words come through.
"He hasn't."
"So, did you ... make up, or what?" A little frustration beginning to creep in.
"Not exactly."

Hardly the apologetic, negative response that I was still half hoping for! I say *half hoping*; I think I had already started to come to terms with the truth. Liz lives for the moment and last week I was *in the moment* for her. She is never going to proclaim an undying love for me in a way which, I now realise, is what I have been waiting for through all these months of disillusion.

"I'll take that as a yes." I despondently assert.
"Ok, if you like; I don't want you to get hurt Andy." She says with some genuine emotion.
I want to say: A bit late for that now though, isn't it? But I don't.
"You'll be better off without me, you know." Liz asserts, prophetically.
"Don't say that Liz. You'll always be part of my life, whatever happens."
"That's sweet of you." She says in a tone that melts my heart a little. We share a brief moment of connection, at last.
"Listen ... I think I'm going to hang up now." I tell her. I can feel a big hole opening up inside me; a hole that is only going to get deeper, the further this conversation goes.
"You know where to find me, if you need me." I add.
"Sure. I'll be seeing you soon enough, I reckon, once I've straightened things out."
"Well, good luck with that." I close with and press the red button on my touch screen.

There's a little regret that Liz isn't rushing over to be in my arms right now, with everything still unresolved. However, all I need is a drink and a half an hour of quiet contemplation to come to an important conclusion: I'm feeling better already!

1

Ok, so I had a couple more large whiskeys to celebrate my new found freedom before I hit the sack but it didn't affect my ability to put in a good shift at the office the next day. In fact the conscientious attention that I applied to a few urgent items at the top of my to-do list seemed to prevent most enquiries as to my well-being. I was totally on top form when I breezed in to Abi's group in the afternoon.

As I'm a little late, there's already a huge amount of energy being generated by all the activity. I can see Abi is engrossed in a read through of the script they are going to be working on. It's early days with the full production not scheduled to kick off until after the summer break but she wants to give the lead players plenty of time to familiarise themselves with the story.

The rest of the group are improvising some dance moves and seem to be having a very good time doing so. With no desire to interrupt them, I head over to see if I can be of any assistance with Abi's group. Surprisingly, she immediately thrusts me into reading one of the parts and entrusts me to continue in her absence as she goes to check in with the young dance group.

After a nervous and hesitant start, I soon realise that her faith is mainly in the cast members who would probably do just fine without me. But, I have to say, I find the whole experience extremely gratifying and the time whizzes by. All too soon, Abi is back to take the reins again and wrapping things up. Eventually, we're able to grab a moment to ourselves.

"That was superb." I say to encourage Abi in the great job she's doing.

"Oh good, I'm glad you enjoyed it. Why don't you take that home with you?" She asks, meaning the script in my hand. "Carry on next week, if you like."

"Ok. I'll make sure I arrive on time." I reassure her.

"Does your face still hurt?" Abi enquires, directly.

"A little but not as much as yesterday; it's nothing to worry about really."

"It must have been quite a shock though?"

"Yeah, well ... sometimes, when you play with fire you end up getting burned." I grudgingly admit.

"So, you're wiser for the experience then Andy?" Abi teases me.

"Oh, undoubtedly." I acquiesce.

Abi breaks off to have a parting word of encouragement to her troop of players and we share a comfortably enjoyable silence making good the room before closing up. In no rush to be anywhere, I join Abi on a nearby bench whereupon she just closes her eyes and basks in the afternoon sunshine. Feeling liberated, I follow suit.

"So, what now?" Abi enquires, still smiling at the sun with her eyes closed.

"Head back to the office and finish up for the day, I suppose."

Abi gives me a glare, "You know what I mean ..."

"I guess I'll try to make a fresh start ... if it's not too late."

"Well, what have you got to lose, eh?" Abi asks, sincerely.

"Not much; as long as I don't end up with a matching bruise on the other cheek!" I jest.

"I don't think there's any chance of that: Mel's nothing if not compassionate. You don't get to be in her job unless you have a good understanding of human nature. Just don't be in too much of a hurry ... give it some time."

I nod and we return to enjoying the warmth of the sunshine once more.

"Thank you." I proffer.

"You're welcome." Abi acknowledges.

"I fancy an ice-cream."

"Good idea." Abi agrees and off we trot.

१

"Fools rush in where angels fear to tread" is one of my favourite sayings, even if I do seem predestined to regularly play the fool. However, on this occasion I heed Abi's advice and give myself a day or two to consider my opening gambit when I speak to Mel. By Wednesday evening, I am composed and ready to take the plunge. At least, that is, until she picks up and begins to speak! My voice cracks and I stumble through a few polite exchanges until, with huge relief, I manage to make her laugh.

Ten minutes later, we are discussing places to go on Friday evening. Mel asks me if I've seen *The Great Gatsby* yet and I admit that I haven't but stay silent on the fact that I wasn't intending to. Honestly, I'd prefer to watch the original version again but this is much more about my relationship with Mel than my interest in the work of Leonardo DiCaprio. So, we have a date!

When I bump into Abi at work the next day, she already knows about it. I start to recognise that there may be some people in my life that are really looking out for me and giving me a helping hand. It makes me feel good about life. And, apart from a slightly cryptic text from Liz about Matt's latest financial exploitation of her, I sail through to Friday evening in much the same vein.

I just have enough time to go home and shower at the end of my working week before heading in to town, where Mel is due to meet me for some al fresco fish & chips in the park. Again, her choice, not mine. Half way through the bag and I think the relaxing ambience of the park bench is working wonders. Mel is merrily chomping away; I am licking my fingers and beginning to look forward to a couple of hours of escapism in a dark room.

Thankfully, after six days, there is little visible evidence of the damage inflicted to my face and therefore no reason to feel self-conscious about my appearance. And so far, I've been steering the conversation towards what Mel has been up to since we last met, a fortnight ago. Inevitably, the lost weekend rears its ugly head.

"I wish I'd been around for Tom and Abi's party though." She affirms.
"Yeah, me too ..." I swiftly reply. If she had, things may have turned out a whole lot better, I was thinking.
For some reason, which I can't quite explain, "... things may have turned out a whole lot better, if you had." I say.
Mel looks a bit nonplussed.
Suddenly, I have an overwhelming urge to banish the elephant from the room: come what may.
"Mel, there's no point in my trying to pretend that nothing happened last weekend ... because I know you know that it did. Nor do I want to insult your intelligence by making excuses."
I pause to meet her gaze; she doesn't have a horrified look on her face, so I continue.
"I just want you to know that, whatever it was that I was thinking, I've realised it wasn't good and it wasn't clever ... and ... I'm sorry."
Now, I can't look up. But, looking down, I see her hand reach out for mine and I feel the warmth of her touch. I like it.
"One day, Andy, I'll tell you something that I know you don't know then you might understand why I find it so easy to forgive anything you might be regretting right now. And I admire you for being honest with me, truly."
Relieved and intrigued, I take my focus away from the delicate fingers that I have been studying and on to the friendly eyes that

have been observing me. There is nothing more to say; we have both acknowledged the others sincerity and Mel breaks the silence by stealing one of my chips and laughing as she slips it into her mouth.

I could get used to this, I really could.

"We've got time for a quick drink in the bar, if you like." Mel suggests as she tidies up the dregs of our meal and looks around for a bin to deposit them in.

"Lead on." I command. If only she knew just how much I needed a drink!

The cinema is in the park, so we arrive at the bar in a few minutes. With about half an hour to go before the main feature there is already a small congregation of film lovers but we manage to get a table in a cosy corner. As we sip our rum and cokes, our surroundings put me in mind of my own working environment and I begin to enlighten Mel regarding my joyful Tuesday experiences with Abi.

"You know, you look ten years younger than you did an hour ago Andy." Mel cuts in.

"Do I? What made you say that?" I ask, a little over defensively.

"You're talking about something you enjoy and it shows in your face; I'm just pleased for you, that's all. But, hey, I should have taken off my psychologist's hat by now!"

"No, it's nice to hear you say it; I was a bit tense earlier on." I confess.

There's a stir in the gathering throng as the doors to the auditorium open. Mel sinks her drink (mine is long gone) and we join the well-mannered and courteous queue to take our seats near the back. It's a full house and there's quite a bit of chatter which we add to by discussing the relative merits of the cinema and the theatre.

I'm just about to make a suggestion when the lights go down and the screen burst into life. It will just have to wait until after the show.

The Great Gatsby is a dazzling success with both of us. Mel says she is feeling quite drained by the frenetic pace of it. I, on the other hand, am invigorated and would happily whisk Mel off to Thursdays in an attempt to reclaim the missing hours from last Saturday. But I content myself in the knowledge that the evening has gone far better than I had expected and I don't want to push my luck. Before we part, I recall the conversation that was cut short earlier.

 "So, do you have any plans for tomorrow night?" I venture.
"No ... no, I don't. What did you have in mind?"
"Well, we could try out the theatre experience if you like. There's a show on called *If Only* which I haven't seen yet: I've heard that it's very funny."
"Ok, funny sounds good." Mel affirms.
"Come over to mine for a rum and coke first, if you like ... say ... 6:30?"
"Sure, text me your address."

And so, with an all too brief embrace, Mel disappears into the gloom of a summer twilight. I am sober and whistling a happy tune as a gratifying Friday evening draws to a close. Or so I thought as I close my door on the world outside and retire to my inner sanctum.

Chapter 9

I wouldn't call myself a curtain-twitcher and I am quite used to the generally good natured revelry that passes by my door as the night people wend their way home, but this time I had to take a peak outside. A lone drunk woman, who has decided that the best place to sing *"This toooooo-oown ... is comin' like ... a ghost tan ..."*, is propped up against the tree just across the street..

A nearby street lamp illuminates her and I am struck by the familiarity of her features. I watch, partly amused and partly bemused, as she tries to maintain some coherence to the lyrics. As she stumbles forward out of the shadow of the tree I can now see that it really is someone very familiar. I'm out of the front door without a second thought and across the otherwise empty street to catch her as she falls.

"Cart gowon no ... maw ..." Liz slurs with a smile.
"Hello Liz ... let's get you inside, shall we?" I recommend.
"Ooooh, Andy, wad ur you doin' ere?"
"Well, I live just here; I thought maybe that was why you picked that particular tree to have a sing song under."
"Yar .. that's right." Liz manages to recall.

I manage to get her arm around my shoulder and begin heading back to the open doorway. As I go, I look up and notice the odd chink of light beaming from behind a slightly pulled curtain. They are extinguished as I peer towards them and soon make it out of view. Shows over; I close the door on that little episode and deposit my guest in to a comfy chair.

I regroup in the kitchen where I'm thinking that this must be some kind of divinely constructed test. But no, that's a ridiculous idea, isn't it? I just have a drunk friend in my lounge and I need to be disciplined enough not to let her stay the night because, well, that's just a stupid idea! There's no way that I am going to line myself up for another bruising my Mad Matt and what would this week have been about if I jump straight in and ..? Well, you know.

Coffee it is then.

I watch Liz trying to rouse herself and get a grip on her surroundings as the kettle begins to boil. The noise attracts her attention and her bleary eyes lock onto me.
"I'm making us some coffee and then I'll run you home." I inform her.
"Oh, that's sweet of you ... can I have a wish-key in mine?" She requests, mischievously.
"Not tonight, eh?"
"Aw, wadever you say master ... you'd take care ov me, wouldn't ya Andy ...?"
Liz pauses to gather her scattered thoughts.
"Not like that good-fa-nofin leach of a boyfrrr-end I lumbered myself with!"
I am totally on her side there but I don't much want to be hear it right now, so I let that one go without comment.
"I bet ... Andy, I bet ... you", Liz points a finger at me, "... will end up with someone reelly, reelly nice."
"Coz you deserve it Andy." She concludes.
"Well, we'll see." I reply as I hand her a strong fresh coffee.
"Thanks. I'm gonna miss you when I'm gone, Andy."
"You're definitely off then?"
"Yeah, HE doesn't like it ... but quite frankly, he can go swivel!" She laughs.
"Does he know?"
"Kinda." She says, vaguely. "You will come and see me, won'cha?"
"Sure thing."

With the combination of the coffee and the chance to unburden herself, just a little, Liz seems to be getting back on a even keel. She goes quiet, rests her head on the back of the chair and closes her eyes.

I stand behind her and rustle her hair. "Time to get you home, I think." I tell her.
"Can't I stay here a bit longer?"
I ignore her protestations and help her out of the chair. Walking her home may be a good remedy for her but I'm not sure if I can handle her over the distance, so I guide her into the passenger seat of my car.
"Matt won't be waiting at home for you, will he?" I anxiously ask.
"He shouldn't be ... but you can drop me outside if you don't wanna come up; I think I can make it up in the lift ok."
"No, I'll risk it. I don't wanna leave you out in the street ... just in case."
And so, we whizz round to her place and, all too soon, she's blowing me a kiss on her threshold and closing the door. Another crazy hour on whatever planet Liz is on right now.

Out in the cool night air, I look up in time to see her bedroom light go out and I'm happy to have been her Good Samaritan once more. But this time, I'm walking away with my sanity only mildly disturbed and the prospect of a peaceful night's sleep ahead.

ۅ

Nice to have a lay in on a Saturday morning, isn't it? Even better when you have a date to look forward to in the evening; better still if you are going to be able to be *Mr Oh-so-popular* by taking your date back stage at the theatre!

With an afternoon to kill, I wander into town. Out of curiosity, I meander past Liz's shop and peer inside to see if she is free. I want the reassurance of knowing that she is ok after last night but it is, unsurprisingly, pretty crowded and I can't see her anywhere. I can make out Bev assisting a punter so I tell myself that everything looks hunky dory and move on.

After browsing a couple of menswear chain stores to see if anything jumps out at me I find myself heading west from the Market Square. The sun is high and I feel the need for a spot to chill for a while. The thought strikes me that the cathedral would be airy and cool so I decide to go in and explore - see what I've been missing out on.

Once inside, the peaceful atmosphere is very pleasant and welcoming. I clock the leaflets but I'm not in the mood to take in all the historical detail; I just want to soak in the good vibes. I guess that the place is several centuries old and there would be plenty to discovery at a later date. The height of the vaulted ceiling in the nave is quite staggering and I chose a seat to take it all in from. Though there are many people milling around me, there is only the softest murmur of voices to disturb my tranquillity as I begin to imagine the generations of worshippers that have had a similarly impressive first experience as mine. Having passed a good twenty minutes in contemplation, I complete a circumnavigation of the rest of the building, culminating in an enjoyable stroll around the cloisters and a cold drink in the cafe.

Hitting the Saturday afternoon cacophony back in the pedestrian precinct is a rude awakening to my semi dreamlike state and it is a relief to reach the end of North Street. The traffic on the ring road is slow moving as people begin to head off home with their fix of retail therapy over for the day. My hands are empty of material goods but I certainly haven't returned without something to enjoy from my trip.

I put on a CD that Abi had lent me a while ago (and had kind of ignored due to the fact that I had never heard of it) because I think there is a chance that Mel might be in to it too. To my surprise, I recognise the first song, Kumbaya, and I start paying more attention to it as I am getting ready for Mel's arrival; I even have a little dance while waiting for the kettle to boil. I pause it after track four and plan to have it playing quietly for when she arrived: my anticipation of which is giving me a very welcome thrill.

I just have time for a micro-waved ready meal before smartening myself up and making the place tidy. Resisting the impulse to start on the drinks prior to Mel joining me, I happily recline with an alcohol free coke and hit the play button with ten minutes to spare. The track number is showing seven when the bell rings. Mel, dressed to suitably impress, glides cheerfully into my lounge and immediately gives it the once over.

"This is very nice Andy." She approves.
"Thanks ... and you are looking very nice too." I reciprocate.
"Thank you." Mel beams a smile at me. "I don't get to go to the theatre very often, so it's a lovely opportunity to dress up a bit."
"Well, make yourself at home ... and I'll pour you a nice long drink; rum and coke?"
"Yes, I could do with one of those, thanks." She says as she complies with my instruction and re-arranges her loose flowing hair; a fleeting image of her beauty is indelibly written into my memory as I try to focus on the task in hand.
"There you go ... one *Andy Special* ..."
 We clink glasses and Mel expresses her appreciation with a thirst quenched sigh after her initial tasting.
"So, what do you think of the *Collective*?" Mel asks.
After a few seconds wondering who she is talking about, I twig that she is referring to the CD and have to confess, "I really like it. It's Abi's: she thinks they're brilliant ... and I can see why now."
"She made me a convert too: she may be on a mission!"
We laugh together and I immediately feel any residual nervousness dissipate. The drinks are helping too, I believe. I suggest that we cross the road to relax with another long one in the Theatre's bar.

We arrive a good thirty minutes before the curtain goes up, but it's already beginning to fill up; obviously a popular show. It feels nice to be on home territory, so to speak, and be greeted with nods and smiles from some familiar faces. However, I'm hoping that our evening together will be an intimate affair, so I take Mel off to a secluded corner.

"You're very lucky to have all this on your doorstep." Mel observes.
"Yes, I know; I should make the effort to do this more often though."
"Well, if you're ever short of someone to take, I'm more than happy to fill in. It makes me feel like a proper grown up when I do this sort of thing: I get so absorbed in the world of children during the week, it's the perfect antidote. Quite the opposite for you though, isn't it?"
"Yeah ... but this is where it all comes together: more like a celebratory glass of champagne than an antidote. When do you get to celebrate?" I wonder.
"Oooh, not that often, unfortunately. Small victories, for sure, but no big parties I'm afraid." She says.
"How about outside of work?" I continue, fishing for a more positive response.
"Hmmm, just the usual ... birthdays and weddings. But I like to think that there is something worth celebrating every day: like a beautiful sunset, someone smiling at you .... or watching a play with a friend ..."
"Well said, I like your thinking." I affirm.
I make that two heavy hints that have registered in my consciousness; I get a strong feeling that we might be doing this again sometime.
"So, what was the last play you saw?" I enquire.
"Well, I'm afraid I usually go with the crowd, so it was *The History Boys*. I think the time before that was *Les Miserable*! So, this one is a complete step in the dark for me."

"I'm sure you'll like it ... and we can have a heated political debate about it afterwards." I jest.

"Oh, I had better pay CLOSE attention then." Mel says, faking unease. "I do hope you're not too right wing ... otherwise we could come to blows."

"Far from it." I re-assure her. "I do have aspirations though."

"That's good: maybe we can talk about those afterwards instead then."

I smile at her in recognition of her interest and watch Mel polish off her drink.

"I'm just going to powder my nose before they call us. Don't go in without me, will you?"

"I'll be right here." I avow and enjoy the last cool mouthful of my beverage in her temporary absence.

The PA announces that the show is about to begin and the orderly rush to take up our places begins. Mel returns in good time and we mingle in with the excited throng. As we go in, Mel grips my hand to ensure that she has my attention.

"Thanks for inviting me Andy." She says in a warm, soft and, to me, sexy tone of voice.

"My pleasure." I freely admit.

Once the performance is under way I glance across to see whether Mel is enjoying the experience and I'm happy to see that she is. My interest in her facial expressions lingers and then wanders into an appreciation of her moist lips, at which point she becomes aware of my attention. Unashamedly, I continue with my assessment and notice the sparkle of the stage lights reflected in her eyes as she looks at me.

Mel returns her focus to the political drama being played out before us without comment or reaction, except the faint ripple of a knowing smile. Any further intrusion on my part would start to feel a little odd, so I too pick up on the dialogue and return to the matter in hand. I allow the anonymity of the darkness enfold me and disappear into the illusion of the story.

When the interval arrives and the applause rings out, the brilliance of the house lights comes as a jolt to my senses.
"Let's have ice-cream!" Mel excitedly suggests. "What flavour?"
The pre-show drinks and the low lit environment don't seem to have affected her in the same manner as me. Quite the opposite, in fact.
"Er ... mint chocolate if they have one, please."
Mel rushes off to beat the queue and leaves me to reflect on the state of our democracy. Of course, I could have done that. Instead, I consider the options for prolonging the entertainment after the show.
Mel's pre-emptive strike is a success; in next to no time she is re-seated and consuming her vanilla tub.
"I was thinking, maybe, you might be interested in taking a look backstage after the show?" I venture.
"Mr Roberts, if you're trying to impress me ... then you have." She coyly responds.
"Oh, no ... I don't want to raise your expectations too high; there's no Champagne party or anything. I just thought ..."
Mel giggles, amused by my retraction, and I cut short my explanation.
"... I'll make sure there's Champagne ... next time." I conclude.

We both resume our consumption of frozen dessert in an easy silence as the hum of conversation from the other spectators fills our sound space.
Mel makes an observation about the play while gleefully scooping the last of the rapidly melting confectionery from the bottom of its cardboard container. I'm still savouring the sweetness of the ice-cream and the pleasure of her company as she speaks.
"... mmmmm, that was lovely ..." She inserts, once the tub has been scrapped clean, "... can I have a taste of yours?"

"Sure." I comply.

Taking a plastic spoonful, I lift it to her mouth and watch it slide in and disappear before drawing it back out. I feel tempted to repeat the process, just for the childlike delight of it all but Mel seems content to sit back and observe the rush of people back to their seats.

The second half is about to begin. For me, the interval has been wildly more engaging than any of the drama that has been unfolding under the stage-lights. A flashback of my lonely bus ride back from the nightclub, just seven days ago, makes the present moment feel even more exquisite. I take Mel's hand in mine as the lights go down and happily allow my senses to slip into the land of make-believe.

For all its commendable dialogue and fine acting, there is a part of me which is impatient for the play to end. Still, I do my level best to absorb the subtleties and nuances; I don't want to look a complete idiot during any potential after-show discussions with Mel - or anyone else for that matter. Not too onerous a task, I should add. In fact, we both join in with our heartfelt applause as the cast take their bows at the end of proceedings.

With the lights up there is the usual release of vocal cacophony after the prolonged period of stillness and an inexorable movement toward the exits. We are swept along but I take Mel in hand, literally, to manoeuvre her toward the VIP backstage experience.

"We need to cut through here." I direct her but Mel doesn't take my lead.

"Can we make it another time Andy?"

"Yes, of course ..." I concede, feeling a tad relieved. "I quite fancy getting some air, to be honest.

"Me too." Mel smiles and performs a nervous little wiggle to convey her pleasure at my response.

And so, in no time at all, we're leaving the crowd behind and I find myself walking the wall, with a girl on my arm and in no great rush to be anywhere in particular at all.

Chapter 10

Oh, how sweet a sound those cathedral bells are making as I awake, home alone, the next morning. My thoughts drift back to the joy of wishing Mel goodnight and I feel reconnected, as I plump up my pillows, when I imagine her enjoying the same auditory experience.

I indulge myself in the notion of Abi eagerly requesting a report when she arrived at church and extrapolating all the pertinent details over tea and biscuits afterwards. But hey, do you know something? I believe I was having a really good time by satisfying my impulses and that rousing from my bleary-eyed stupor the next morning is the proof. How liberating to feel that, just maybe, a new chapter of my life is beginning?

Even on Monday morning, my new found optimism seems to elevate me to a level of greater enthusiasm and efficiency. But whoa, down to earth with a bump I come before the sun was over the yardarm.

As I waxed lyrically to one of my fellow workers about the play, in an effort to motivate their interest in going along themselves, I am interrupted by another who says I have an urgent phone call to take back at my desk. Even this somewhat alarming intervention does not register in my consciousness as anything to concern myself about or dampen my zeal.

"Hello, Andy Roberts speaking …" I introduce myself.
"Hi Andy, it's Beth … from the shop …"
"Oh hi, what can I do for you? I hope Liz hasn't gone AWOL again." I joke.
"Erm, no, much worse this time …"
"Really? How come?" I ask, with a more soberly tone.
"She's been taken in to St Richards … she's OD'd Andy." Beth blurts out with considerable emotional impact.

Momentarily stunned, I half manoeuvre and half collapse into my office chair and stop myself from rolling into the wall as my momentum propels me backwards. I manage to keep hold of the phone and something in my head stops me from uttering my usual profanities.

"Whoa, what did she go and do that for?" I ask Beth, rhetorically.

"You'd probably know that better than I would Andy."

"Yes, I suppose I should but …" But what? Why was I struggling to accept the possibility? I couldn't complete the sentence.

Beth realises that I'm incapable of any further coherent response and fills me in with the details.

"I spoke to her father this morning and he had just come back from the hospital. I think he'd been up all night, the poor man. Anyway, the good news is that she's out of danger now and he says she'll make a full recovery. It'll take a day or two before they'll look at sending her home though and he'd prefer it if she didn't have any visitors today."

"Ok, gotcha." I affirm and relax a little as the information sinks in.

"I guess I'll just have to run the shop as best I can in the meantime."

"Yeah, do whatever you need to do … and thanks Beth."

"I'll not visit her: I don't like hospitals. Give her my love and let me know how she is, would you?"

"Yes, sure."

"Ok, well, you know where to find me …" Beth concludes.

"Yeah, I'll be in touch. Take care."

I listen to the dial tone for a few seconds as my immediate surroundings re-establish themselves in my consciousness.

A couple of nearby faces are looking in my direction with a concerned expression on them. One is sufficiently aware of the solemnity of my demeanour over the last few minutes to enquiry after my well-being.

Wishing not to elucidate but grateful for their kindness, I say that I'm fine but think it would be best to take an early lunch and so, I leave the office.

Outside, life is progressing to its own familiar rhythm and it seems at odds with the calamity that is eating me up inside. Walking away from the Theatre and in to an area of open space, the reality of my ex-lover laying in a hospital bed breaks through all my English reserve and I am reduced to sobbing whilst pressing myself against a nearby tree. How cruel to be prohibited from rushing to her side to take her under my protection?

I play back the events of Friday evening in my head and search for some point at which I could have or should have seen this coming. Then I berate myself for having such a great time on Saturday night when Liz, to my mind, may have been longing for me to call. But once I've finished beating myself up and the tears had dried on my face I take to sitting with my back to the majestic oak and just staring up at the sunlight through the rustling leaves.

These are the tears that I'd been wanting to cry since she left me behind in the Lake District, I think to myself, and smile.

Somehow, I manage to do something useful with my time in the afternoon and leave work after everyone else had gone home. Being at the office with other people felt emotionally stabilising but I now find the quiet empty space hard to vacate.

But leave it, I must, and in the shadows of the lobby I notice the figure of a man who looks suspiciously like Matt. My heart almost stops as I move towards the exit and he turns around. Seeing his unfamiliar features is such a relief that I said "Hello" as I breeze past him and on into the fresh air. The idea of having to deal with the man himself is now festering in the recesses my mind though. I walk straight to my door with one desire: to shut it behind me, turn off my phone and pretend not to be at home.

After an hour or so of staring at the ceiling, from the comfort of the sofa, the one clear thought that I have is that it must have been an accident; I just don't see Liz as someone who would have tried to end it all in that way. Whether it was some badly cut coke or a genuine mistake I didn't know but I really hope that she can now see what she has been putting herself through. And if it was a cry for help, then I would have be there to listen … but no more.

I ring out for a take-away and watch some TV. It crosses my mind to ring Mel, not to talk about Liz but just to hear her voice and hear about her day. In the end I decide against it though. No need to over-complicate things, I think.

∫

No need to hit the booze either; I am thankful of that the next morning. I am kinda thankful that Liz is on the mend and I can go in to see her later on too. I pop in to the shop to have a quick chat with Beth at lunchtime. There are a few details I want to check with her … like where to find Liz for starters … that I had been unable to ascertain yesterday. Of course, I want to make sure that she is doing ok too.
She sounds a little on edge, not knowing just when Liz will be coming back, so I tell her I'll return tomorrow to talk things over. It is all I can offer, in the short term.

After that, I go in search of Abi. I'm not in a good place for engaging with her Tuesday group and I need to talk to someone that I really trust. I know that she'll be there early to set things up so I just wait for her and enjoy the solitude. Enjoying the solitude again, what has got into me?

I think it may have only been about ten minutes before Abi's cheery face looks in and I see the satisfaction of finding me here pay across it. My contemplations up to that point have led me to a little revelation about where my troubles are based and where the

114

answers are coming from. Abi's first sentence seems to sum it all up nicely.

"Glad to see you're here early Andy, I think today's going to be a lot of fun ..."

But then she clocks the apologetic look on my face and realises that all is not well.

"... but I guess not, for you Andy?"
"No. I'm sorry Abi but I'm going to have to give it a miss; something's come up." I lamely explain.
Sitting down next to me, Abi puts a comforting arm around my back and waits for me to elucidate.
"I'm ... er ... going along to the hospital later, to visit Liz."
Abi's face remains attentive as I struggle to continue.
"Apparently, so I've been told ..."
I'm finding it hard just to say the words.
"... she took an overdose."
"But she's doing ok." I hasten to add. "I can't tell you much more, I just don't know what happened. She turned up at my place on Friday night, pretty wasted; I sobered her up and took her home but didn't think she was about to, well, you know, do something like that."
"Try to take her own life, you mean." Abi frankly states.
Taken aback by her clarity, I can only affirm, "Yeah." For the first time, I allow myself to concede the faint possibility that this may be the truth.
"Andy, I haven't known you very long, but what I've seen and heard of Liz makes me think that she's lost her way somewhere and now she's looking for it in the wrong places."
Nicely put, I mentally acknowledge.
"And that's why I feel so involved ... responsible even, maybe; she got lost when she left me!"

"Oh Andy, I really don't think you believe that, do you?" She suggests.

"I think I did ..."

"But not now?" Abi prompts me to say it.

"No, not now ..." I agree, "... but I still want to help her out."

"And why wouldn't you? You're a good friend." She declares. "But if you want my advice, you need to let her find a better way ... so that she can be a good friend to you."

There's a long pause while this sinks in.

"I do need to see her though; she'll want to tell me about it and I want to hear for myself."

"Yes ... definitely, you go. Let me know how it goes." She requests.

"Will Mel understand?"

"Have you not worked that one out yet?" Abi teases me.

I give her a perplexed look and add, "I guess not ..."

Abi shrugs and leaves me to ponder.

"Buy you some lunch tomorrow?" I offer.

"Sure. I best get ready, they'll be here soon."

With that, I slip out and head back to the office, wondering just how it's all going to pan out.

Thankfully, the time spent waiting proves to be a fruitful and I'm not left clockwatching. With only a ten minute walk to the main entrance of the Hospital, I'm looking on the board for the Acute Medical Unit before I really have time to mentally prepare myself for our imminent reunion. I guess I'm trying to avoid over-thinking the whole thing; I'm just visiting a friend who's had an unfortunate accident, after all.

Eventually, I manage to locate the correct bed in the appropriate bay in the relevant ward and am pleased to see that Liz is sitting up in the high backed chair by her bed rather than on some kind of life support. From the looks of it, she's just eaten half of a meal from which she didn't much care for the mash potato.

"How's the food in here?" I jovially enquire by way of a greeting.

Liz looks up and ignores my question due to her obvious delight at my arrival.

"Andy! I'm so glad to see you ... I'm going insane in here."

I bend down to receive a brief hug along with a peck on the cheek.

"They want me to stay in another night but I feel fine Andy, I really do."

"Well, they'll most likely want to make sure you're fit to go home, Liz, so just go with it, yeah?"

Liz looks a little disappointed that I'm not taking her side, so I carry on.

"I'd like you to fill me in on what you've been up to, exactly, since I dropped you back home on Saturday morning but hey, I'm just happy that you're ok."

"Of course I'm ok!" She protests, quite unexpectedly. "I overdid it a bit, so what?"

"Ok, ok ... I knew that would be it; still a big shock to the system though, isn't it?"

Liz doesn't have an immediate answer so I search around for a free chair to pull up and sit down, facing her, for a little tête-à-tête.

"A nasty shock for me too, you know?" I continue.

"Well, yes, I'm sorry about that: at least you care, unlike *some* people ..."

I presume that she is referring to Matt.

"... he hasn't been in touch at all Andy ..."

The story unfolds.

"... not since he walked out on me."

"And when was that?" I enquire.

"Saturday evening. I was pretty strung out after my little visit to your place ... so I wasn't that keen on repeating the process. But Matt came over and got all arsey that I'd been to see you and wasn't up for going out with him."

"Yeah, I was on the lookout for him yesterday." I interject.

"I think you'll be ok. Like I say, he's keeping a very low profile."
Liz looks pained and tired as she contemplates the meaning behind her statement.
"You see, it was his idea to do a couple of lines together … to *perk me up a bit* … as he put it. Trouble was, he'd really done my head in, losing his temper again and I wasn't in the mood for dragging around with him: so, he just stormed off, telling me he'd *had enough of this.* So, I just thought I'd take the rest of the gear that he'd left behind in the heat of the moment … and have a much better time without him!"
I can guess what's coming next but I wait for her to verbalise it.
"And that's when things got a bit unpleasant … until eventually I … threw up and passed out. I did manage to call Dad at some point though. Apparently, I wasn't making any sense so he came over and found me on the floor."
She lets out a nervous giggle, which I can't comprehend.
"What's so funny?" I need to know.
"My Dad." She replies, but I'm none the wiser.
"He's full of surprises."
She sees my confusion.
"I'll tell you later."
She smiles, I move on.
"Ok, so, when do you think they might let you go home?"
"When my stats are normal … which they aren't yet, so they say; I feel a bit rough still but I put that down to being stuck in here. Anyway, I won't be going home straight away: Dad's taking me in for a bit of convalescence, bless him."
"That'll be good … give yourself time to think things through a bit." I suggest.
"Maybez." She muses. "You will come see me again, won't you?"
"Of course! Why wouldn't I?"
"Well, I haven't been at my best recently." Liz admits.
"Perhaps not … but we still have more to talk about, don't you think Liz?"
She doesn't commit herself by replying.

"So, how about, you come over to me on Friday and I'll rustle something up?" I propose.

"Ok, I'll bring a bottle."

"Wine … not coke!" I jest and Liz laughs: much to my relief.

"Just like old times, eh, Andy?"

I see in her eyes that asking this question has a slightly melancholic effect on Liz and I don't have the heart to say what I'm really thinking.

"Yeah, just like." I concur.

"You're looking well Andy." Liz candidly states. "You must tell me what you've been up to: but not now, I'm feeling a bit drowsy. I think it's my medication kicking in."

"Ok, I'll head off home; any messages for Beth before I go?"

"No, I think my dad's handling any issues with the shop in my absence. Just thank her for being cool about everything … and I'll make it up to her when I get back, I promise."

"Right. I'll love you and leave you then." I pronounce and give her a kiss on the forehead as I do so.

Walking back out, down the hygienically clean corridors, I can't help wondering: when IS Matt going to show up again?

Chapter 11

The next morning, I receive a text from Liz to say that she has been given the all clear and her dad is on his way to collect her, which she is very happy about. I dutifully call in on Beth again during my lunch break and she is very happy about it too. I don't have to explain anything to Matt, so I am really, really happy about that.

Thursday is a mercifully peaceful day. The desire to socialise seems at odds with my basic need: to evaluate all of the events and conversations that I have been a party to since my arrival. An evening of summer sun in the garden is enough to keep me happy, with a freely delivered pizza and a couple of bottles of Premium Italian Lager.

There is a part of me that constantly requires some kind of calibration and I sometimes wish there was a reset button that I could press but, as I enjoy the sensations of the air cooling and light fading, I feel that the future is bright. In spite of my own anxieties and dis-inclination to settle for any length of time, which I freely admit to, I can see that there is the distinct possibility that I may be about to experience something new and heavenly in a relationship.

Coming in from the dark, with a real sense of connection to place and time, I decide that there is only one thing to do ... ring my folks! Dad answers and we exchange a few pleasantries before he passes me over to mum. She is much more interested in how I am doing and I tell her as much as I can: work is going well, I've made some new friends etc, etc. When asking about Liz (whom she's never met but knows that we'd been happy together) however, I find myself becoming less free with the truth. We agree that it is high time that I came to see them and I say it would be good to have them over some time too; just not yet.

Finally, after switching off my bedside light and lying awake for some time, I can't free myself from the pangs of guilt that have beset me after talking to my mom. I resolve to set things straight for the next time, bring her down and let her see for herself just how good my life is in West Sussex.

And so, I manage to get to sleep, ready for the day ahead: Friday.

Liz confirms that she has recovered sufficiently from her ordeal to join me for the evening and that her Dad will drop her off around seven o'clock. This gives me plenty of time for last minute preparations ie shopping for the weekend and getting started on the sumptuous meal that I intend to dish up. She tells me that she'll be going back to her place *afterwards* … and my intension is to ensure that she's there before things get out of hand.

At five past seven I hear her father's Range Rover pull up outside and the door open. Peering through the lounge window, I can see daddy imparting some words of wisdom to his wayward pride and joy before she descends from the passenger seat and the door clucks. She waves him off and I'm there to let Liz in before she's made it to the threshold. I give her a welcoming hug and in return she hands me a bottle of Shloer.

"I'm under orders, Andy: full detox. I hope that's ok with you."
"Yeah, no problem. Good for you Liz. You're looking much better; are you feeling ok?" I ask, as we move on through to the kitchen and pour a couple of glasses of the White Grape.
"Aw, it's nice of you to say that; if only you knew how long it took me to get ready … us girls have to look our best!"
"Looks can be deceptive though." I suggest, in an attempt to elicit a more informative statement regarding her well-being.
"Andy! Are you suggesting that under all this slap I might be hiding the real me?" Liz drolly protests.

I sense that Liz is uncomfortable with verbalising the answer to my question and I let hers hang in the air as I set to my culinary endeavour by boiling the rice. The pregnant pause in conversation seems to disarm Liz a little and she finally sheds some light on matters.

 "That's going to take more than a bit of make-up, Andy."
"But no amount of drugs, heh?" I boldly propose, in hope of her assent.
"I guess not."

I'm pleased to hear it but Liz doesn't say it with any sense of conviction, more in resignation.

"Let's not talk about that now, eh?" Liz pleads and wanders outside to ensure that her wish is granted.
"Let's eat out here." She shouts back to me.
Popping my head round the corner, I see Liz is pacing the garden with a fag on the go and leave her with her thoughts as I test that the rice is cooked and serve up chicken chasseur à la Roberts, for consumption al fresco.
Liz has taken a seat at the table on the patio once I emerge.
"Here you go." I proudly present my offering.
"Smells fantastic; I always did enjoy your cooking Andy." Liz responds and we slip into a less intense reminiscence of a time when things seemed much less complicated.

On one level, I was enjoying the chance to re-live the good times but on another, it is making me more aware than ever of our emotional separation. For a while, it appears that Liz is oblivious to this inescapable truth but eventually she opens up to me; just like old times!

"Yesterday ..." She begins.
I feel like singing, *"all your troubles seemed so far away"*, but I resist the temptation.

"… I had a long chat with Dad; I don't think he trusts me to start again, on my own, right now."

"Oh." I simply respond: sitting on the fence while intrigued to discover what comes next.

"He said he'd given me the benefit of the doubt over the court case and I'd convinced him that everything was going to be alright in the long run. But this time, I really put him through it … and I reckon he just wants to keep me close by until he's sure I'm back on the straight and narrow."

Liz washes down another mouthful of chicken with a large draft of grape juice before revealing more.

"After all he's done for me, I can't argue. Do you know, he drove me to the hospital himself and *actually* went to clean up my flat afterwards? All the time I was on that ward, I was waiting for someone to say that I needed to answer a few questions but they never did; it's as if it nothing happened … which feels a bit weird, to tell you the truth."

More chicken is consumed. "This is great Andy." Liz enthuses.

"So, you're going to play ball this time?"

"Well, like I say, I don't have much choice: I feel an obligation, kind of thing." She concedes. "I'll do whatever I need to do but …"

Chicken and juice break.

"… I'll level with you Andy: I just don't like anybody telling me what I can or can't do, right. I know Dad wants the best for me." She pauses and takes a tangent. "Unlike Matt, who so obviously doesn't give a damn, right now!"

I'm left reeling at the vehemence of her outpouring but even more aghast at what follows, after finishing the last of her rice and refilling our glasses.

"Anyway, all this has got me to thinking that I should have stayed in the Lakes with you; all I want to do now is get back to something I already had."

"Seriously?" I wonder, with a hesitancy born out of disbelief.

"Well, why not? You're the only bloke I know that isn't always on my case … and anyway, isn't that what you came here for?"

There is some truth in what she asks; however, that was then and this is now.

"That may be so …" I begin my argument but to no avail. Liz gets up without any concern for my intended reply and offers me a hand.

"Let's go inside and make ourselves more comfortable." She suggests with a *come hither* look.

I take her hand and my heart is racing: not in anticipation but in the knowledge that a significant event in my life is rapidly approaching. My body may be compliant but my mind is set on a different outcome. And as for my soul: it has been on this road to nowhere one too many times and is screaming out, *Enough already*!

"Liz, wait up." I assert and cut short our progress through the ground floor on route to the first. "This isn't why I asked you over."

"No? Well, it's why I came."

"Then I'm sorry to disappoint you. Yes, you're right; I did follow you down here but I wouldn't have needed to, if you'd stayed. Things are different now; I like this place. I'm making a life for myself and I think it's going to work out ok." I declare.

"So, all your calls and texts, they were all a big mistake, yeah?"

"I wouldn't say that, no." I counter.

"And spending the night in my bed: was that before or after you had this change of heart?" She assails me again.

"Hey Liz, you know me better than that?"

"Oh, do I? Not anymore, apparently." She concludes as she snatches up her bag and heads for the exit. "I'll send you a postcard Andy."

Dazed, I remain standing in the middle of my lounge for several minutes after the front door slams. Clearing away the remains of the meal gives me something to distract myself while I calm down but, at the end of the day, I'm not feeling too bad: I've said it now and that's that.

∫

The same cannot be said for Saturday. My natural tendency towards self-recrimination and the sun shining in on me by five in the morning sees me heading to the kitchen for a reviving cup of tea. I'd woken up to a very rousing and enthusiastic dawn chorus but I was finding the birds' joyfulness at odds with my own mood and, therefore, somewhat irritating.

It didn't take long to reacquaint myself with the possibility that I might have been pulling Liz's warm torso closer to mine; the only way that I can break my train of thought is to get up and stick the kettle on. I throw on some loose clothing and my Crocs then wander out the back where, apart from the birdsong, all was calm, peaceful and at odds with my memories of the night before.

Surveying my property, mug in hand, I become emboldened by the pleasure that's felt through just being in my own home and acknowledging that I had exercised my right to chose. I had chosen to move my life forward and I wasn't going to apologise to anyone for it. The next step, I think, will be to share these emotions with a trusted friend. But it is still only six o'clock in the morning, so I go back to bed for a bit!

Showered and shaved, a couple of hours later, I strike on the novel idea of ringing Abi to ask if she feels like joining me for breakfast at a suitable venue in town. She is very pleased to be invited and suggests a place that she likes down in Southgate. I look in, just as the bells begin to chime another hour, and spot her sitting under a picture of Audrey Hepburn.

"Good morning." She cheerfully greets me as I take my seat.

"I do hope so." I quizzically reply.

"Why shouldn't it be? Look, it's Saturday morning and there's a whole glorious weekend ahead of us."

"Oh, I do love your positivity Abi."

"I have a lot to be thankful for. But so have you Andy."

"I guess so."

"You *know* you do." Abi rebukes me and then adds, cryptically, "Maybe more than you think."

"Well, there's more to life than what you own. I like to think that a bit of honour and decency goes a long way: the old Corinthian Spirit and all that."

"And I do *love* that about you Andy."

"Not always easy though." I confide.

"Hold that thought Andy; let's order some breakfast and you can tell me about it."

My full English and Abi's bacon roll take a few minutes to arrive. While we wait, the hot tea sufficiently lubricates my brain and vocal cords to begin: an expurgated version of the tale of Friday night. Abi remains impassive, excepting a brief interruption for the application of brown sauce when I get to the finale.

"So, do you have any regrets?" Abi incisively enquires.

"A few." I pause for effect as Abi takes a bite without getting the joke. "But then again ..."

Now, she chuckles. "Seriously Andy."

"Well, for starters, it's not a great feeling when a friend decides to walk out on you like that."

"Nor to be the one left behind." Abi suggests.

"No ... and that's it really; she's been consistently leaving me in her wake. Even though I do wanna give it another try, I just know I'd be left high and dry again at some point."

"Pearls after swine, Andy."

"It's what?"
"It's a well known verse, from the book of Matthew; chapter 6, I think."
"Oh, really?" I respond, with guarded nonchalance. "Got any more words of wisdom?"
 "I don't think you need my advice Andy, you seem to be working things out ok on your own." Abi re-assures me."
"No pain, no gain, eh?"
"Is often the way, I'm afraid."
A comfortable silence envelopes us as we tuck in to our morning feast.
Abi starts the conversation up again but on a lighter note. "Did you know that there's a lot about Corinth in the Bible?"
"Vaguely; never read it. I've seen all the Greek stuff at the British Museum though."
"It was part of the Roman Empire then." Abi continues.
We contentedly fall into the consumption of bacon, once more.
"So, what are you going to do with the rest of your day?" Abi asks as she polishes off her tea.
"Oh, I thought I might head down to Wittering for a swim. Come with me, if you like."
"I'd love to Andy; we're visiting Tom's parents though."
"Another time, maybe." I conclude.
"Not thinking of inviting Liz, are you?"
"Nah. Quite fancy a nice relaxing time on my own, to be honest." I affirm.
"Ok, well, must dash."
"Ok. Don't worry about the bill … my treat. Say *Hi* to Mel for me." I implore her.
"Great, thanks." Abi says as she kisses me on the cheek. I stay a while to enjoy a renewed sense of sanity along with a fresh cuppa.

∫

One lazy Saturday later: one whole day has passed with neither Liz nor I brokering a truce. It doesn't sit comfortably with me but I'm determined to ride this one out. What I really want to do is to ring Mel and see if she's free this afternoon. The familiar peel of the Cathedral's bells reminds me that she'll probably be in church with Abi and my curiosity is awaken as to what is passing between them, beyond my simple greeting.

In a moment of peaceful contemplation, I reach for my phone and do a search for the keywords *Corinth* and *Bible* to see what comes up. In less than a second, I have close to a million references on the internet: enough to keep my interest for a little while.

After browsing a few of the historical interest sites and getting a pretty clear picture, I come across an online Bible site and touch on the link to take me in. What I find is a letter, not the Bible story that I was half expecting. Chapter 1 is hard going and there is more of the same in Chapter 2. I give up in Chapter 3 but I feel that I had learnt a little something about Mel, somehow: which isn't a bad thing. A little knowledge can go a long way, I think.

It is looking like another good afternoon to get out and about, so I drive over to the Marina for some time down by the water and a look at the yachts. I pass by Tom's on the off-chance that they may be about to set sail but there is nobody aboard.

On returning, I have a very nice surprise: Mel rings to enquire after my welfare. She also apologises for ignoring me all week, on the grounds that she'd had a rough week at work. Yesterday, she'd thought about me while visiting a friend in Brighton. Today, she has been in town and tried to pay me a surprise visit but I hadn't been home, unfortunately. However, as we are both free now, she says, would I like to come over to hers for a little something. Stopping off at the garage for flowers delays me slightly but I am there within an hour, eager to partake ... in *something*.

Thankfully, Mel loves the flowers and rewards me with a kiss for being so thoughtful. Chrysanthemums are one of her favourites, she says, but thinks it is early in the season for them. I agree, trying not to show my ignorance and watch her as she arranges them in a vase.

Mel's focus on the task in hand allows me the opportunity to study her, unobserved, as we chat. The self-confidence she exudes and the casual beauty of her persona give me a strong sense that this is a moment to savour. At the completion of her floristry she turns to me, meets my lingering gaze and sashays over to me.
"You like?" She asks.
"The flowers? Yes, you could have a whole new career there."
"Were you looking at the flowers?"
"Well, not when there's something more beautiful on view." I respond; stirred, but not shaken.
"Correct answer, Mr Roberts."

From which point, everything goes rather well, I must say.

We drink a bottle of very good Rioja while I do my best to relate the story of my week. I get the feeling that she may have heard some if it already but she doesn't let on. She lets me go on though with a sympathetic, if not empathetic, air. I try not to deviate from anything that I'd told Abi; I even made light of Friday night's events as, in all honesty, I did feel that a burden had been lifted from me.

Much to my relief, we do not dwell on such matters. Mel simply relates some of her professional insight as we share some bread and cheese, washed down with a second glass of red.

Much more to my satisfaction, we stop talking altogether as the sun sinks below the line of the trees outside; communication on a whole different level occupies us until the light is shining horizontally on to the wall and reflecting off a line of framed pictures.

Despite the alcoholic lubrication everything remains serene, if not a little unruffled. The intense emotional experience of crossing into a deeper relationship with Mel leaves me contentedly laid out on her sofa as she gets up to brew up a pot of coffee.

With Mel comfortably nestled into my shoulder we enjoy the rich aroma and a silence envelopes us in the fading light. Eventually, I break our peaceful enchantment.

"So, can I see you again next weekend?" I ask with an expectation of approval.
"Oh, I expect I can find some time from my hectic social whirl."
"Any chance of going out with Tom and Abi on the boat, do you think?" I wonder, with no expectation.
"I don't know; want me to ask?"
"That would be great." I enthuse.
"We're doing a puppet theatre practice on Sunday, if you fancy joining us for that too."
"Yeah? How could I help?" I hesitate.
"Oh, you're a man with many gifts: I'm sure we can put you to good use."
"What's the show about?"
"Good question Andy! It's about Paul, The Apostle, and his time in a Roman prison. Doesn't sound much fun, does it? But it will be; trust me."
"I do Mel, I do."

Chapter 12

By lunchtime on Monday I'm desperate to get out of the office and into the summer glow that says to me, *England in July*. It seems like a good opportunity to take a stroll over to Mel's place and drive my car back. Last night was not the time to be getting pulled over for drinking and driving, so I did the sensible thing and enjoyed a moonlit walk into town.

My route took me past Liz's flat and a fleeting urge to kiss and make up had risen up in me as I did so, but in my heart I knew that I should just walk on by and I quickened my pace: onwards through the Eastgate. It's never that simple though, is it? One final tug on my heartstrings was just around the corner, nonetheless.

This time I am an unwilling pawn in, what seems to me, some kind of farcical sitcom; it is probably more akin to a tragic TV drama but is, in fact, reality for Liz. It's as if the whole weekend was just the interval and the second half of the performance unfolds when she re-enters, stage right, and we return to our positions: seated at the table in my back garden.

"Look, Andy, I was really out of order the other night." She apologises: which is a good start.
"Yes, you were Liz." I agree, in a non-committal sort of way.
"But you forgive me, yeah? I just wasn't expecting you to turn me down like that."
"Of course I do but …" I am unable to complete my sentence.
"No. No *buts* Andy. I just wanted to know we were cool before I go."
"Go? Go where?"
"Cornwall. I told you: I need to get out of here." Liz insists.
"I thought you're dad was against that idea now."
"So what? I'm not going to stick around just to please my dad and Matt."
"And how did that go down?" I dare to ask.

"Dad came round to the idea, eventually. I said I'd give it a month; see how it goes. It'll be great, I just know it."
"Well, I really hope it works out for you."
"It would work out better if …" The sound of the doorbell cuts Liz's sentence short and her mood changes dramatically.
"Expecting anyone?" She enquires, suspiciously.
"No. Are you?"
"If it's Matt, I'm not here, right."
"Ok. If it's Matt, I don't wanna be here either!" I jest.

It's Matt.

"Oh, hello Matt. Long time, no see." I nervously greet him.
"Cut the crap Andy. Where is she?"
"Who's that?"
"Who'd you think?"
"If you mean Liz, last I heard she was at her dad's." I lie. "Is she not there now?"
"Well, her car ain't. It's just over the road and it's packed with her gear."
"Oh, she might be anywhere Matt. You not spoken to her recently?" I attempt to clarify.
"Nah, I've … well … she was all over the shop: I've stayed out of her way for a bit." Matt confesses and I almost want to invite him in.
There's an awkward silence as neither of us know what to say or do next. Until, that is, I have an urge to be honest with him.
"Look, I could help you out Matt … but the last time we met, you made it very clear to me that I should stay out of your way, so …"
"Yeah, I did, didn't I." Matt grins and throws a mock right hand in my direction.
Well, an apology would be nice but at least he's smiling, I console myself.
"Ok, nuff said." Matt concludes and starts to walk off.

I watch to make sure he's really gone before closing the door and breathing deeply behind it.

"So you hadn't told him." I confront Liz with this revelation.

"No. Why should I? He's history. In fact ..."

"Okay, okay; I get the picture." I interject, having heard enough already.

Liz calms down and re-evaluates before resuming.

"Thanks for not letting on Andy. I appreciate it ... and that's kinda why I wanted to tell YOU Andy: coz if you're not coming with me then I hope you'll be paying me a visit before too long, yeah?"

"Maybe. Send me a postcard."

"Yeah, I will."

∫

Ok, on reflection, *happy* might not be the best way to describe my mood on Tuesday. The need to just get on and do my job presents a pleasant distraction from the swirl of emotions that has engulfed me over the last forty eight hours. Indeed, the disturbance in my equilibrium is such that I manage to forget what day it is and fail to turn up for Abi's group in the afternoon.

True to form, she's patient and kind: accepting my apologies without asking for any kind of explanation, which is nice.

For the rest of the week, my head is in a different place altogether and the dream of jacking it all in to be enjoying the Cornish coast, either with Liz or doing my own thing, really does appeal to me. As the days drift by, I get to a better handle on how blessed I am with what I have right here, right now.

I tell myself that I don't have to let go of that dream. Now that I had a solid base to work from I just need to start planning for the future. Maybe what I need are some more dreams to chase after, not less.

By close of play on Friday, I am itching to get home and get the weekend underway. But first, I think I'll drop in on Abi to find out if the boat trip is on for tomorrow. To my great joy, it is. We need to be up early to catch the morning tide. I am glad, I can't wait.

Once indoors, I get changed and try to relax. The itch won't go away though. Now, I want to out again. So, I go to the chippie and sit on *our bench*, as I now consider it to be, and consume my fish in deep contemplation. I sense that I am on the threshold of something new and it feels a little scary.

I take a good look around me as I munch my way through the last of the chips. All of a sudden, the penny drops and I realise that I have found what I was looking for. I am already part of a bigger and better dream: I have finally let love into my life.

Now, there's just one question I want an answer to: where is that going to take me?